MONICA TIN

THE LATE MRS. PRIOLEAU

MONICA MCLEAN TINDALL was born in 1907, of Anglo-Irish ancestry.

After attending Oxford University in the late 1920s, she was sent abroad by her parents to get over a man they considered unsuitable – nonetheless, the suitor, Brian Campbell, became her husband in the following decade. The couple happily spent the rest of their working lives as school-teachers.

Monica Tindall's sole novel, *The Late Mrs. Prioleau*, was published in 1946. She died in 1999.

MONICA TINDALL

THE LATE MRS. PRIOLEAU

With an introduction
by Gillian Tindall

DEAN STREET PRESS

A Furrowed Middlebrow Book
FM13

Published by Dean Street Press 2017

First published in 1946 by Peter Davies

Cover by DSP

ISBN 978 1 911579 31 1

www.deanstreetpress.co.uk

INTRODUCTION

WHAT AN ARRESTING first line for an otherwise modest and reflective novel! – *'The first and only time I saw my mother-in-law was when she lay dead in her coffin.'* Following the classic rule of detective fiction that when a body appears early in the story a murder is being signalled, you might expect a sinister du Maurier-style tale of evil and retribution. However, this book is far more of a quiet study of bygone relationships and of the lost world of Britain before the first World War, as seen in the context of the further social upheavals brought by the Second.

It was published in 1946, so evidently written while the War was still continuing: its time-frame runs from early in 1939 to the on-going London blitz in the late summer of 1942. Its first person narrator, Susan, is a young New Zealand woman who has come to an England without family or friends, having recently married an English naval officer who is inevitably absent much of the time. The purpose of this is clearly to make it credible that Susan should have her first introduction all at once to a whole dysfunctional family, and then find herself drawn into assisting them in various ways and getting to know them: she is an available person with no one else dependent on her. This works, in that we can absolutely believe in Susan's suppressed irritation with Austin, the dead woman's fat, spoilt, middle-aged son, her patient ear when the dead woman's doctor and man of business variously confide in her, her more irritable desire not to be told things by a gossiping house-keeper or a long-retired maid, and her gradually developing relationships with Austin's two sisters and with an elderly aunt, sister to the dead woman. The cumulative effect is a little repetitive, and the plot device by which Susan comes upon a cache of letters in a locked dressing case that no one else knows about is not really very plausible. But the assorted information is so skilfully leaked, and the descriptions of by-gone places and times so vivid and convincingly real, that one turns the pages eagerly to piece together more knowledge of the lives that are being bit by bit revealed.

Monica Tindall herself came to regard the book as weak in plot construction. I know this because she told me so. She was my aunt, and the Anglo-Irish family history on which the novel draws is mine too. I recognise many echoes in it from assorted manuscript memoirs, particularly those of Monica's own mother, my paternal grandmother. By the time I knew her this grandmother, married for many years to an English medical publisher, regarded herself, with humour, as 'a fair imitation of an upper-middle class English matron', but she was a good raconteur and when launched on reminiscences of her youth her intonation would relapse into that of Dublin rather than the Home Counties. The family had been, for generations, country surgeons and then fully qualified doctors; thus they occupied very much the position of nearly-but-not-quite-landed-gentry that in the novel is occupied by the Crawfurds with their whiskey distillery. My great-grandfather avoided the sudden religious fervour ('poor Father's peculiar illness') that is the financial downfall of the fictional family, but he did die suddenly and before the younger ones among his too numerous children were yet launched on the world. My grandmother, though reared to Presentation balls in Dublin Castle as Helena is, had known the anxiety of penury and the need to seek a genteel paid role as a companion. Her providential marriage in 1905 to the son of her late father's prosperous publishing contact was certainly arranged for her, although, unlike Helena in the novel, she became devoted to my grandfather and they led a pleasant and hospitable life together.

And yet ... Her daughter Monica, once adult, did not have an easy time. Her generous father allowed her to go up to Oxford, something he himself had been denied and that not all fathers did permit their daughters in 1927. There she met, as was to be expected, a young man of suitable education from an acceptable Scottish Public School – but once he had finished at Oxford he was without resources and emerged into adult life in the depth of the 1929-30 economic recession. He was also, not surprisingly in these circumstances, a socialist. Monica's parents determined that he Would Not Do as a prospective husband, and over the next ten years huge amounts of emotion, plus a certain amount of money, were expended sending Monica to remote corners of the Empire in the ill-founded belief that she would thus 'get over' Brian and meet someone better able to provide her with a comfortable life-style. No doubt their intentions were good. But it was a peculiarly silly fixation, given that Monica was a genuinely intellectual, rather determined girl who would have been quite unlikely in any circumstances to have made a worldly match. At the same time she loved her parents and did not want to hurt them.

Traces of the grief and conflict this engendered appear in *The Late Mrs Prioleau* in the form of Rowley's inability to provide suitably for Helena if she were to run away with him, and in Helena's own conflict at the thought of abandoning her children. A trip Monica was sent on to Canada provided copy for the fictional daughter Norrie's ill-fated elopement with a French Canadian soldier; and something of Monica's own sense of isolation in the 1930s no doubt fed into the alone-ness of the fictional Susan. Eventually, at the outbreak of war, Monica and Brian, by then clandestinely together in Edinburgh, got married there 'by declaration' and that was that. Probably it was the relief of this, plus Brian's subsequent absence on army service, that released Monica to write her novel.

After the war they found no difficulty in getting teaching jobs together in the world of little boys' boarding prep schools, in which career they happily spent the rest of their working lives. And of course Monica's parents became reconciled to the situation and even quite fond of Brian. The world had changed. But it was the long delay before they were finally together that probably cost them the children of their own they might otherwise have had. Monica undoubtedly loved and admired her mother: the ageing, vituperative Helena is in no sense a portrait of her. But even as a child I sensed that Granny could be quite tiresome, sometimes deliberately combative. Long after her mother's death Monica once said to me: 'Oh – Mother was a destroyer ...' I was too struck by this intense and out-of-character remark to ask further questions, and now all concerned are dead and gone themselves.

The nuances of character, class, conversation and especially place are so surely portrayed in the novel as at once to beg the question: why no further ones? Why did the writer who brilliantly conveyed the atmosphere of an old house near the river Thames by Hungerford Bridge not use her undoubted talents further? (The house, Monica once told me, had been a real one she had visited during the war. Today, its site lies somewhere beneath the South Bank complex). The answer, just possibly, lies on p.18, where Susan mentions her half-career as a detective story writer and remarks that she 'does not like to make capital out of other people's misfortunes' and perhaps lacks 'the credulity to believe in my own fiction sufficiently to make it interesting'. One might express it another way by saying that Monica was that rarity, a writer with more talent than ambition – too many would-be-writers have these qualities the other way round.

In old age, when she and Brian retired, she did try her hand at several more novels, but by then the personal drama that had obliquely fuelled *The Late Mrs Prioleau* was long in the past and she was living a life of conscious peace and comfort. She also wrote poems, which were genuinely good but lacked some edge of pain which would have made them that much better. Writing had become for her a fun-occupation, without the necessary rigour to succeed. She did not really understand this when I tried to explain it to her, though she was generous and interested where my own books were concerned. Once she said she had always wanted to know me better and I was stuck for an answer. I had never consciously maintained a distance between us, but I suspect that what she was picking up was the difference between the lifetime writer, with the necessary touch of ruthlessness, and the person whose life is essentially centred elsewhere.

Gillian Tindall

PART I
THE DISTORTING GLASS

CHAPTER I

[I]

THE FIRST and only time I saw my mother-in-law was when she lay dead in her coffin. Beside her knelt Austin, her eldest son, his face buried in a wet handkerchief and his fat body shaken by sobs. The patchy spring sunshine flickered against the drawn blinds and outside a wind from the sea blew thinly over the marshes. The air in the bedroom was at once cold and stuffy, smelling of damp and illness and old clothes.

Austin was crying without restraint on a high falsetto note like a woman and I found myself wondering how long his waistcoat buttons would support his grief, how long before his handkerchief would actually start dripping.

Henry, who had called me upstairs, looked at him with sick disgust. "He's having hysterics or something, Susan. We've got to get him out of here. He won't take any notice of me."

"Speak sharply to him then." Austin was evidently beyond kindness or reasoning. Henry bent down and shouted in his ear. "Get up now, Austin! Stop it at once."

The wretched creature answered with yet another heaving sob, and Henry poked him with his foot. "Oh, God!" he said with angry patience. "We can't leave him like this. He'll be ill."

I put my hand on the fat, shaking shoulder. "Get up, Austin! Get up now!" The sobbing broke on a long shudder. "Austin! Get up!" I pulled his hands from his face and wiped it with Henry's handkerchief. It was vast and mottled and puffy. He must have been crying for hours.

"What you want," said Henry, "is a stiff whisky and a sleep. Get up!" Like a meek and downtrodden child Austin rose and walked with his brother to the door. I heard him sniffing rhythmically as he stumbled downstairs.

I stayed behind because I was interested. The dead woman was Henry's mother, and I knew so little about his relations that I looked at the body with as much curiosity as though it were a family portrait. She had Henry's dark hair, hardly touched with grey, and there was something of him in her heavy well-shaped nose, but her full mouth with slightly parted lips was not like his, nor the shape of her eye-balls showing large and rather prominent through her closed lids.

She did not look as if she slept. To me she simply looked dead, with every expression wiped from her face so that there was no telling what kind of woman she had been. Only the folded hands retained their character. They were soft and boneless-looking, with spatulate fingers worn and coarsened at the tips, and veins showing blue through the mottled ageing skin. They were the hands of an artist and a gardener. They looked to me somehow cruel in spite of their softness.

Did I think all this at the time? Possibly not. Imaginative reconstruction of one's thoughts and emotions is always easy, especially to a novelist, and this happened long ago. I only know with certainty that I was quite unmoved. Mrs Prioleau was as much a stranger to me as any dead woman could be, and I could only have mourned her if her death had hurt Henry. But Henry had hardly seen or heard from her for ten years, and when he wrote to tell her about me she had not even the manners to reply. She had been an indifferent mother to him as a boy, and although he did his dutiful and decent best he hardly managed to pretend even to himself that he had been fond of her. I think he was sorry she was dead mainly because he felt obliged to attend her funeral.

When I first met Henry I was amazed that anyone who was neither an orphan nor a foundling should be so completely detached from his relations. That he had a mother I knew, and when I asked him if he was an only child he admitted to an elder brother and two sisters, and even told me something about them, but in an uninterested way, rather as though he were speaking of people whom he had once met in an hotel and had not cared for much. His father, a doctor in London, had died when he was still at school, and a godfather, now also dead, had been responsible for his going to Dartmouth and had paid part of the fees. And that it seemed was all there was to know.

I owed so much to my own parents and I had missed them so terribly when they died that Henry's disinterested attitude made me feel rather sorry for him, as though he were stone-deaf or colour-blind. I felt cheated too, on my own account, because I knew so little of what had gone to make him the man he was. What had he looked like before he could walk? What had life been like for him when he was a child at home? I had no one to tell me, to show me the family album and say what a clever baby he had been.

Somewhere in the house now was Austin, and on the road to Wiston were the two married sisters I had never met. They were all older than Henry and must remember him as an infant in arms, but their memories would be no substitute for his mother's, and the little boy that he had once been had died finally with her.

A shrill voice from down the stairs broke suddenly in on the silence. "Austin!" it called. "Austin!" Then came a low, rather malicious chuckle which made me think I was not going to like Henry's sisters. "Draw in now," said the voice on a gentler note. "Draw into the fire and warm yourself." I went downstairs wondering that they had arrived so silently and that I had not heard them talking to Henry.

"Fine morning!" An uncertain tenor voice greeted me. "Fine morning!" Through the open door of the kitchen Mrs Prioleau's grey parrot looked at me with a hard, yellow eye and chuckled. "That parrot!" Henry appeared and threw a cover over him. "How they put up with him I don't know. I hated him when I was a child, and I think he's worse than ever now." He pressed his hands to his forehead. "I've got him to bed," he told me. "Austin, I mean. Talked an awful lot of nonsense, poor chap."

We went into the sitting-room, and a tangle of fat, black pugs who were lying together in a large and elaborate basket rose with a furious yapping. When I went near them they bared their teeth and cringed away. One of them tried to snap.

"Austin's livestock," explained Henry. "I believe he shows them. Vicious little beasts, aren't they? Why doesn't he go in for *dogs*!"

He crossed to the wireless, turned it on and then snapped it off again. "Better not, perhaps. God! what a dump!" The room was cold and the grate empty so that we could not light the fire. It was nearly as uncomfortable as a station waiting room. "What a long time it seems since breakfast!" Henry said sadly. "It hasn't changed a bit. I remember all this stuff in the old house when I was a kid. Susan, why should anyone want to make an ostrich egg into a pincushion and stick it on the back of two silver wolves?"

I looked at the monstrosity. It needed dusting badly. Indeed the whole room needed it. The wan sunshine was thick with dust and the pile of the turkey carpet was flattened from lack of sweeping.

It came into my mind suddenly that we might be living in the first chapter of one of my own detective stories, the kind of story I always felt to be so improbable. A woman lay dead upstairs waiting to be screwed down; in another bedroom a man was having hysterics; in the kitchen a grey parrot was imitating both their voices; and in the sitting-room crouched the pugs, glaring at us now with rage and terror in their popping eyes. Soon a car would drive up and Henry's sisters would join us, and Mr Galvain the man of business; and I, the stranger in the family, wearing black for a woman I had never known, sat in this unfamiliar cheerless room waiting to meet them.

Leonora was romantic, romantic even in Henry's bald biography of her. Leonora had run away to Canada after the last war with a handsome officer, and her father had cut her off and no one heard of her for years, and she was mentioned in hushed whispers as "poor dear Norrie . . . tut-tut." And then one day she came home again, a famous modiste with her picture in the *Tatler* and her hats featured in *Vogue*, and fifteen years of her life behind her of which she never spoke. I thought that I would be interested to meet her.

"What's Melissa like?" I asked Henry, feeling miserably sure that at least one of his sisters would be the image of Austin.

"Oh, all right. I haven't seen her for ages. She designs wallpapers or something. Lord, I wish they'd hurry. I'm starved."

"Henry, she's not like . . ." Hunger and chill were making my spirits fall very low.

"Oh no. Not a bit. Austin's a changeling. You'll rather like Norrie, I think, and Mellie's not too bad when you get to know her. As for old Galvain, well, when I knew him he was like something left over from the 'Cries of London'. Don't you worry, Susie. Everything's going to be quite all right."

[II]

Sure enough everything was all right. Five minutes later Henry's sisters arrived, driven by Melissa in her car, and on their heels came Mr Galvain who had taken a taxi from Chichester Station. My husband greeted them with enthusiasm. "Now we can have lunch," he said. "Straight away."

Despite a certain tension in the atmosphere it was a much less trying meal than it would have been in a more normal family. The resident maid had gone home in a fright as soon as Mrs Prioleau was dead, but the charwoman had provided cold beef and pickles, some sticky-looking jam tarts and a large pot of strong tea, and everyone was hungry. Leonora, whom they called Norrie, had thoughtfully brought a bottle of sherry and some whisky, because "however you feel about it a funeral's pretty awful, and you might just as well feel as little bad about it as you can." She drank two large whiskies herself as a start, without bothering to explain that she had got chilled in the car, and the rest of us had some, except Mr Galvain, who drank sherry with a fastidious expression.

No one seemed to be particularly sorry that Mrs Prioleau was dead, nor to expect that anyone else should be, except poor Austin who had lived with her.

"Asleep," said Henry when somebody asked where he was. "He's a bit tight, poor chap. Best thing for him, and for everyone else."

"Shell shock, Mrs Susan." The old lawyer addressed himself to me. "The last war you know, very sad."

"Shell shock!" Austin's younger sister spoke with an edge on her voice. "He always dodges everything unpleasant by staging one of these scenes. We all know that by now."

There was an uncomfortable pause. "Sleep is the best thing for him anyway," said Mr Galvain. So Austin was left to sleep on while we ate and the undertaker's men put on the lid of the coffin. Henry, after a decent show of reluctance, had two helpings of meat and looked quite disappointed that there was no cheese. It takes a good deal to put him off his food.

There were five of us for lunch, Norrie, Melissa, Mr Galvain and our two selves. Norrie Campion, plump and suave, and dressed in black that looked quite unlike mourning, was anxious that her new sister-in-law should not feel neglected. She addressed most of her conversation to me and provided a running commentary on everyone else's remarks. She asked me how I liked England after living in New Zealand, and how I had enjoyed the voyage over, and didn't I feel mad with Henry for bringing me to a show like this, and wasn't it perfectly barbarous to drink strong tea with beef and pickles, and so on and so forth. Everything she said was trivial enough, but she made it sound important and interesting, and she made me feel important and interesting too. I liked her.

Melissa Hillier was totally different. Her black was as smart as Norrie's, but the line of her dress was hard across her throat, and her black toque hid her hair with a hard line over the brow and ears. Her thin figure and her sharp voice grated on the eye and ear, and her look seemed to turn the world into a laboratory of human experiments organised for her benefit. She treated us all with a faintly irritating benevolence as though she were patronising slum-dwellers, and her grey stare took me in from the crown of my head to the sole of my foot.

"I can't think why you came," she said to me. "It's a terrible way of meeting relations, and you never knew Mother. I don't know why Hal dragged you here."

I said of course that Henry had not dragged me, and promptly felt she suspected I was a necrophile. She would never realise that I would willingly go to a funeral every day of my life simply for the pleasure of being with him.

Mr Galvain was kind. He made a charming little speech when he was introduced to me, and said the nicest things about Henry, though he insisted for no apparent reason on calling him Eustace. He ate his luncheon like an elderly and dapper bird, and he had a soothing manner like a family doctor of the old school. He had evidently attended funerals for years, and his conversation was a model of tact, in this case entirely unnecessary. His aim was to avoid silences, presumably lest anyone should be overpowered by grief, and into any pause, apparently by force of habit, he let fall a suitable funerary comment. "Very sudden. . . . Of course it was only to be expected at her age. . . . Poor Austin! Poor fellow! Happily no sorrow is eternal . . . Well, well! I hope we may all go as quietly when our turn comes." His stock of platitudes seemed quite inexhaustible.

Nobody took much notice of him except Henry, who asked how Austin would be affected financially since their mother had lived on an annuity. Whereupon Mr Galvain's soothing voice became businesslike, and he said that as we knew, of course, she had left everything to Austin, and that if he wished to continue living at Greenbarns it would be just possible, though in his opinion the house was rather too costly. Melissa said that anyway Austin would need a keeper, wouldn't he? And Mr Galvain with a small reproving cough replied that a good sensible person would, he thought, be required. He added, somewhat ambiguously, that these troubles came to us all.

"How's Stephen these days, Mellie?" enquired Henry politely as we were lighting our cigarettes.

"I divorced Stephen eighteen months ago," Melissa replied in her small cold voice.

"Oh!" Henry's jaw dropped slightly. "I'm sorry."

"Very sad," murmured Mr Galvain. "Most unfortunate."

"You needn't be sorry." Melissa ignored him. "We hadn't been getting on well for a long time and were far better apart. It's better for the children, too. They would have been getting old enough to notice soon." She gave a little whickering laugh. "As a family we aren't altogether successful in our marriages. First Norrie and now me."

"What about us?" Henry demanded.

"You've time yet, but maybe you're all right. You're normal. You got away from our happy home early enough." She looked at poor Mr Galvain who was sipping the last of his tea in a disapproving manner. "Our poor father would have turned in his grave, wouldn't he?"

There was an uncomfortable silence. Then the old lawyer recovering, drew out his watch and said we should be going.

The funeral was timed for two-thirty. Henry collected Austin and tidied him, and got out his old Morris from the garage. "You'd better come with us Norrie, I think." She nodded, whispering to me that poor old Austin liked her better than Mellie. So Mr Galvain and I went with Melissa in her aggressively cheerful-looking sports car. Austin had been given another whisky by Henry and a bromide by Norrie, and though he looked like a walking corpse he was composed. He was dressed in the old shooting jacket and flannel trousers that were evidently his normal wear, and his shaving had been done with a shaky hand. His face was swollen with crying, and his dry dust-coloured hair blew in the wind. He seemed utterly lost, like a stray dog in a crowd. Henry murmured something cross in my ear about "making an exhibition of himself" and "shouldn't have come," but he stayed by him and protected him firmly from Melissa, that student of human nature, and from Norrie who wanted to give him more bromide.

The church was nearly three miles from Greenbarns by the road, and as our cars followed the hearse with decorous slowness through the winding muddy lanes, we had time to begin quite an interesting conversation about my late mother-in-law.

Mr Galvain had known her as a bride, and had done all the family business from marriage settlements to wills, and in his dry professional way he mourned her sincerely. He said that when you reached his age and the friends of your youth died you seemed to lose a little piece of yourself each time. "I suppose," he said, "hardly anyone now remembers her as she was when I first knew her. Let me see. Austin is forty and Leonora must be forty-two. It's a long time ago." He shook his head sadly, mourning not the old woman that we were burying but the young one whom he had once known.

"She was a charming girl when I knew her, positively charming, and most accomplished, though she had never been properly educated . . . just the usual smattering. She made that old house in the Kennington Road into a—what shall I say?—a sort of boudoir, full of flowers and birds and toys."

"She was very young?"

"Not twenty. I was a young fellow then, and I was half in love with her, I think."

"Was she pretty?" I asked, and felt that Melissa's unspoken comment was: "Humouring the old man! Why bother?"

Mr Galvain considered. "Well no. Not exactly. But she was bright and warm. Her Irish blood, I suppose. Life quenched her," he added with a sigh. Life had quenched her indeed. The dead face looked as though in life it had never known sweetness or laughter.

"I wonder what made her such a quarrelsome woman." Melissa spoke without rancour. "You noticed the wreaths, Susan?"

Yes, I had noticed them and had been surprised that there were so few. She had lived for five years at Greenbarns, and yet no one in the district had known or cared for her sufficiently to pay her memory this slight conventional tribute. There was a wreath from Henry and me, of course, and a spray of pink roses from Norrie, ("I disapprove of wreaths," said Melissa truculently,) and a small prim circle of laurel and white rosebuds from Mr Galvain, and a large cross from Catherine Lestrange ("Kitty"), Mrs Prioleau's elder sister who had arthritis and lived in Oxford.

Only two other people had sent flowers. There was a rather bedraggled little offering shaped like a heart and made of wilting white tulips and bunches of shamrock that was probably clover, and inscribed in a spidery and uneducated hand: "Dear and honoured Mrs Prioleau. From your aff. old servant Mary Spencer." Beside it was a huge and expensive affair in white lilies, a floral tribute if ever there was one, with the legend: "In Christian and forgiving memory of Helena Prioleau."

"I wonder who was the cat who sent the anonymous one?" said Melissa. "It's so rich-looking that it must have been intended as coals of fire."

"You think it was a cat?" The ghost of a smile flickered on the face of Mr Galvain. "Well . . . er . . . So do I. I mentioned it to Austin and said I thought we ought to remove the inscription . . . in fact, I think we might do so at the graveside . . . but Austin took it apparently quite at its face value. He never will admit that his mother was at times . . . er . . . slightly difficult, especially as she grew older."

I asked about Mary Spencer, the aff. old servant, and he thought he remembered her. "She was before your time, Melissa. Austin or Leonora might recall her. She came from Ireland with your mother, and I rather fancy she married a constable. Yes, that was it. She was a pretty girl with red hair and a nice pair of ankles. Fancy my remembering that now! It must be forty years ago."

"I don't think they should have flowers at funerals," Melissa said, pursuing her own train of thought. "If it's worth worrying at all about the feelings of the dead, Mother would have hated a lot of lilies and things left dying on her grave. After all, she was an artist of sorts, and a gardener. Personally, I think she would have far rather been buried in her own garden. She could do some good there."

"A commonsense view, undoubtedly," replied Mr Galvain in his dry voice. He was just as shocked as Melissa intended him to be, and I was shocked too for a different reason. It seemed so sad that Melissa in all honesty should have no feeling whatever about her mother's death. And my kind Henry had just the same dispassionate attitude, though he was less indecent over it. I wondered again whose fault it had been that the dead woman's younger children could grieve for her so little, while her eldest son was stricken by her dying, and the servant girl of forty years ago mourned her still.

[III]

The funeral was a grim affair as a funeral must be. The churchyard was sodden with the rains of winter and a chilly wind touched with salt blew from the flats beyond the dyke. The clergyman's cassock flapped round his legs like an awning, and he hurried through the service in a low voice thickened by a cold in the head. At the end of the ceremony he shook hands with us all with a mutter of sympathy, and hurried away as soon as decency would allow. He spoke no word about the woman we had buried, and I had the impression that he regarded us all with suspicion and disapproval.

Only two mourners beside ourselves had appeared at the church. They were a man and a woman, both very old and very black, and the clergyman had barely turned his back before they bore down on Austin from either hand. The old gentleman walked with a stick and laboured slightly over the rough grass, but the little old lady darted with surprising agility at her prey. One small black hand held a handkerchief, but if she was crying it can only have been from the coldness of the wind for her voice was aggressively cheerful. Reaching up she pecked at his cheek.

"Poor Austin!" she said. "It is Austin, isn't it? Why, goodness me, how fat you're growing! I hardly knew you." Poor Austin looked at her blankly and his lip began to quiver. With great presence of mind Henry interposed himself and addressed her as Cousin Liza. She gave him a little peck too, and then seeing me, kissed me on both cheeks.

"My dear Norrie, how young you look! How nice! Well, Henry. Your poor Mother and I didn't get on. In fact I hadn't seen her for thirteen years, not since she wrote me that terrible letter. But still you know, blood is thicker than water, and when I saw her death in the *Times* I said to Miss Straker . . .

You know Miss Straker, Austin? . . . 'Well, I never did believe in carrying hatred beyond the grave, especially as you never know who you may have to be on speaking terms with, and so if I take the train into Chichester then I can get the bus on, particularly as I want to see the butcher anyway'."

Henry, slightly overcome, said that it was most kind and he was sure Austin would appreciate it. Then he turned to fend off the old gentleman. Cousin Liza addressed herself inescapably to me with a mild and feline sweetness. Obviously she wanted to have all the fun of hating my late mother-in-law and all the fun of forgiving her at the same time.

"Your poor dear Mother, Norrie dear. That was an *awful* letter she wrote. And after all I'd done for her. I cried my eyes out over it for three days. Still, we were good friends once you know." She sighed. "Sadly changed! I sometimes think . . ." She pursed her lips and nodded with a wise expression, and the bunch of shiny black grapes on her hat nodded too with a small rasping sound.

"You liked Canada?" she asked me. "I thought you were still there."

I managed to convey to her that I was not Norrie, but before I had identified myself she had turned and was kissing Melissa warmly.

"It was very sudden, wasn't it?" she said. "You didn't expect it, did you? It must have been a terrible shock to you all. After all, as I said to Miss Straker, your mother's your mother whatever she may have done."

"It was heart," replied Melissa coldly. "Austin found her dead in bed when he went in to say good-morning."

"As sudden as that, was it? How dreadful! What a shock for the poor boy! He must feel so lost without her. But I suppose he always knew it would happen one day."

"A sad business . . . very sad." The old gentleman was addressing us impersonally in an unctuous voice as though we were a public meeting. "I hope poor Helena repented before she was called to her account."

"Oh—er—I expect so," Henry answered obligingly. "Susan . . ." In spite of vagueness about his family he could rise remarkably well to a crisis. ". . . this is Mr Septimus White, an uncle of ours by marriage. This is my wife, Susan, Uncle Septimus."

"She did me a great wrong," boomed the old gentleman relentlessly, "a very great wrong."

"Oh! I'm sorry about that."

"So am I, but I never harbour malice."

"Quite right. Not worth it," Henry agreed.

"I came," Uncle Septimus continued determinedly, "because I believe one should forgive."

"Of course, of course. You've seen my sisters?" But irritation was wasted upon Uncle Septimus. He refused to be side-tracked from his mysterious grievance. "I hope they don't take after your poor mother. One should not speak ill of the dead I know, and I am a religious man who never cherishes any ill-feeling, but I am bound to admit that had my principles been less rigid I might well bear malice."

"I am very sorry to hear it." Henry turned impatiently and began moving to the churchyard gate.

"Quite, quite. And as I have told you already, I forgive her utterly . . . utterly. But if you were aware of what I have had to forgive . . ." He blew his nose dramatically and looked round for a fresh audience.

"And the parrot's still alive?" Cousin Liza was asking Norrie. "It used to talk so amusingly, I remember."

"If you were aware of what I have had to forgive!" repeated Uncle Septimus White. Norrie asked him what it was and he looked pleased. He had evidently been waiting for the question.

"When your poor Aunt Louise died I married again, and your mother took up a most offensive attitude. She said that everyone was talking and that it was tantamount to committing . . . er . . . adultery. Why, I never discovered, except that it was maybe a little . . . soon."

"You were probably not very comfortable as a widower?" suggested Melissa, with the expression of one prodding a rat to see if it was dead.

"No," agreed Uncle Septimus gratefully, "I was not." He drew a deep breath. "Well, she has gone to her last account." He blew his nose again expressively.

"And now," Norrie said brightly, "this is where we say goodbye. It'll take you all your time to catch that bus. Most kind of you to come." She shepherded them to the road and her voice was the soothing voice that she uses for difficult customers. "Yes, yes. I'm sure she would have appreciated it. Yes, you catch it in the village." As they hurried off she remarked that she hoped there *was* a bus.

"And which of the two old cats sent the coals of fire, Susan?" Melissa murmured reflectively. "Gush or Unction? What a pair!"

"Oh, Cousin Liza isn't a bad old thing," Henry said. "You remember, Mellie, she used to send us Easter Eggs."

"I think she used to look after us sometimes when Mother went away. I just remember it." Norrie frowned thoughtfully.

"She took darn good care to let everyone know that Mother had written her a rude letter and she was being forgiving about it." Melissa turned suddenly on Austin. "Austin, did you know anything about Mother writing letters to people?"

"N—no," said Austin, coming out of his trance of misery. "No. Certainly not." He had a faintly guilty look, as though Melissa had accused him of writing them himself. Mr Galvain, who had been very silent, gave him a queer look over his spectacles, and murmured: "De mortuis nil," and Melissa observed that it might be someone else who had sent the wreath, because a number of people seemed to dislike Mother, didn't they?

"Oh, do be quiet about the wreath," said Norrie, suddenly irritable. "We're all sick and tired of it."

In this atmosphere of general faint ill-humour we parted from Henry's relatives. We shared Mr Galvain's taxi to the station, leaving Norrie and Melissa in charge of Austin and the two cars.

"She'll manage him all right," Henry said, referring to Norrie. "They were great friends when we were kids. I've told her to make him drunk again if she has any more trouble."

"Poor fellow!" murmured Mr Galvain. "Poor fellow! I've asked Lorton to come in tomorrow and see how he is. I think he should go away for a while, but he refuses to leave his little dogs. Dr Lorton is his doctor, Mrs Susan, and a very old friend—a friend of his father's and my fellow trustee. He's in good hands."

As we rattled away in our taxi the two cars overtook us, the sports car driven by Melissa and then the Morris with Norrie driving. Austin sat by her, but though she waved to us he did not even turn his head. He looked as flaccid and inert as a badly stuffed doll.

CHAPTER II

[I]

DURING THE NEXT few months I was somewhat involved in the affairs of Henry's family. I was a stranger in England, with no friends and no anchorage except Henry, and while he was with his ship I was a good deal alone.

I had no more time than I could spend in exploring what to me was a new country; but I had far more time than Norrie, with her hat-shop in South Molton Street, or Melissa with two children and her work—she was an interior decorator. As a result, I was asked to do several small jobs in connection with my late mother-in-law, and I learnt a number of things about her which I would otherwise never have heard.

My first expedition, out of which everything else arose, was to Mr Galvain's offices in Chalmers Street, off Lincoln's Inn. Henry was in the North Atlantic, and one or two small matters had to be settled relative to his mother's estate. All that she could leave, including her house and furniture, she had left to Austin, but there was some stock in which she had only a life interest and which had to be divided among all her children. Henry had given me power of attorney and I went to Mr Galvain's office to sign some transfers.

I was not prepared to find him in a very modern office, but this was the kind of office that I thought had disappeared even in England, up three flights of mousy-smelling stairs in a Dickensian room full of files and little black boxes with names painted on them and large pieces of mahogany. The elderly clerk who admitted me sat at a desk in a small, dusty, hutch-like room by the door, and he wore steel-rimmed spectacles and scratched away busily with a quill pen all the time I was doing my business. When I looked out of the window I half expected to see the coach for York roll by with the squat form of Mr Squeers on top wedged between two of his miserable pupils.

In his familiar lair, in front of a bright and over-hot fire, Mr Galvain looked younger and larger than when I had seen him before. He asked after Henry—by his right name this time. And when we had done our business he gave me a glass of sherry and a cigarette with several arch old-gentlemanly jokes to the effect that if he were a few years younger he would be showing me round London himself. Finally he invited me to do him the honour of taking luncheon with him. "Nothing remarkable of course, Mrs Susan, but some place where perhaps you have not been before. Their game pie is excellent, by the way."

We stumbled down the mousy stairs and out into the April sunshine which lay in pale dusty bars of yellow on the lanes and alleys of Chalmers Street. London sunshine is so different from the bright, clear sun of New Zealand or the softer light of the English country. Even in spring, when there is no warmth or strength in it, it has a sort of body. It is thick with dust and the smell of petrol and flowers and rubbish in the gutter, and it lies like a wash of solid colour on the ugly grey buildings and the dingy streets. Mr Galvain came out into it blinking like some small human animal from a children's book, drew a deep breath and rubbed his hands, and said: "Ah! Quite spring-like!" in a voice of profound satisfaction, and when we passed a flower-seller he made a charming little speech about spring flowers for the spring of life and bought me a bunch of violets.

We had lunch in a queer little restaurant behind a spectacle shop with a case of glass eyes in the window, and a very good lunch it was too. We had soup and some of the famous game pie, and because it was, as my host said, "an occasion," we drank claret, and he and the old waiter made a tremendous ceremony over warming it and drawing the cork.

Before I married I made a living of a sort as a reporter and a writer of detective stories. I was not especially successful because I have neither a thick enough skin to make good capital out of other people's misfortunes, nor credulity to believe in my own fiction sufficiently to make it interesting. But I still see people as "copy" though I no longer make my money out of them, and deduction is as much a game with me as it was with my own pet detective, Ambrose Honorius Barty, now mercifully defunct. I still try to discover the job of the man beside me in the bus by the Holmesian method of looking at his coat sleeve and the toes of his boots, and almost unconsciously I interview the people I meet, trying to ask them the right questions and sort out the answers.

Without realising it, Mr Galvain probably talked to me a good deal more than he would have done to most clients under the same circumstances, and by the time I left him I had learnt a good deal more about my husband's family than

Henry had ever thought to tell me—indeed probably more than he knew about it himself. Mr Galvain took a frank pleasure in the sound of his own voice, and once started he went on almost without prompting, meandering like a gentle stream through the quiet reaches of his own early life to the more turbid waters that were the family history of the Prioleaus.

He admitted to having been slightly in love with Henry's mother, and for his father he had had a profound admiration. Henry remembered him chiefly as an irritable person who came in unexpectedly and grumbled because the house was noisy, or cross-examined his children with laborious heaviness on what they had learnt at school. Mr Galvain remembered him as a younger man, before ill-health and disappointments soured him, before he realised that his marriage with Helena Crawfurd was an utter failure.

William Prioleau had been, as I knew already, a doctor of medicine. He was a deeply religious man to whom his profession was a mission, and he did his duty in the dirt and poverty of a slum practice in Lambeth long before the ameliorations of pensions and health insurance. He had been working there for fifteen years when he married, and he died in harness, a worn out old man, when his youngest son was thirteen years old.

Pneumonia killed him in the end, but for a long time he had suffered from rheumatic and gastric trouble produced by incessant overwork. He was so tired for years before he died and he had lived so long surrounded by wretchedness that he had lost all knack of being happy. He had neither the energy nor the inclination to play with his children or plan treats for them, and it seemed to him that they should be so thankful for the blessings of warm clothes and good food and higher education that they ought to expect nothing more of life.

Henry, as a man, realised that his father had been a good and conscientious doctor, and was impressed at the time of his death by the number of poor patients who came to the house. "He was the poor man's friend," they said. One old man held him by the elbows and told him to pray God earnestly to make him a worthy son of so good a man, advice which he did not take. He had heard far too much about being made worthy, and his faith in prayer had been badly damaged some time previously when he was given Southey's *Life of Wesley* for Christmas instead of a bicycle.

"That was his tragedy," said Mr Galvain. "He loved children, but somehow he never could be on comfortable terms with his own family. Long before these Child Welfare Clinics and such were established he was wearing himself to death to get them set up, but I think his children—it seems rather a dreadful thing to say, but I am afraid it is true—nearly disliked him."

The old man finished his claret, and continued thoughtfully, picking his words. "In my life I have, of course, had good opportunities for observation, and it seems to me that in a—er—difficult marriage the children are particularly liable to cause disappointment to their parents. I am not referring here to the inevitable friction in a family where the parents are actually on bad terms, but to the simple fact that, whatever may be said of the influence of environment, children, in my opinion, inherit much of their character ready-made from their parents. Now if the parents themselves are ill-assorted—shall I say, mentally incompatible—it stands to reason that the children of the marriage are likely to have characters, or rather tastes and inclinations, out of sympathy with one or the other parent. At the same time the parents, disappointed in each other, turn to their children and either overwhelm them with affection that is denied other outlets—I am afraid the late Mrs Prioleau did this to his great detriment in the case of her elder son—or else make impossible demands upon them. William expected his wife to be a companion and an echo of himself, and when she failed him he asked the same of the children in the nursery, and they failed him too. Really, of course, he had a most dominating nature, but he was quite unaware of it, poor fellow." Mr Galvain sighed. "He thought," he added with unconscious sarcasm, "that he was giving them a Christian education."

He looked slightly shocked when I smiled at this last remark. "He was a good man," he said reprovingly, "a wonderful man in spite of his faults, and he was a wonderful doctor. I worked with him on legal matters in connection with several of the hospitals at one time—of course I was some years his junior—and I saw a good deal of him. I had the highest opinion of his character and ability."

For half an hour by the clock, between thoughtful sips of his port, or leaning back with his finger-tips together, the old gentleman told me of Henry's father, and his tales gave me for the first time an idea of the old London of cabs and gas flares, and of the work of a doctor among the poor of those days. Drink and tuberculosis were two of the scourges, and Dr Prioleau fought them fanatically, not only with his black bag and his professional skill, but with his right arm and a knob-ended ash-plant. Crash went the stick through the tight-shut window of the consumptive, and crash went his fist against the jaws of the drunk and disorderly. It was, he said, far less trouble for him to knock them out at the beginning than to let them start fighting with bottles and have to stitch them up later in the cells. Providence and the affection of his patients saved him from injury in these affrays, and by night and alone he could go where even by day the police walked only reluctantly and in couples. He had been a more remarkable man than his children knew.

"But he should never have married," said Mr Galvain. "Poor Helena!" He glanced at the clock with a sudden realisation that for one of his profession he had been talking perhaps indiscreetly.

"My dear Mrs Susan, I apologise! I have kept you an unconscionable time. You must forgive me. I like talking, and when you get old there are so few people who will listen to you. And I still have something to speak to you about, if you can spare me a moment longer." He blew his nose and began to speak in what I was beginning to recognise as his "business voice."

"It is about Austin," he said and paused. "Dr Lorton and I—I should explain that he is both the family physician and my co-trustee—consider that it may be—er—advisable for Austin to leave Greenbarns, and Lorton is particularly anxious for medical reasons that while he remains there he should not be surrounded by relics of his mother. He himself terms the poor fellow a serious case of fixation, and while I rather dislike this psychological jargon, on the whole I am inclined to agree with him in this matter on financial grounds." He paused again and I wondered what was coming.

"Leonora and Melissa are very much occupied," he added lamely, "especially at this time of year." Another pause, during which I gathered what he was trying to ask me.

"We feel," he said—"I have spoken both to Dr Lorton and Leonora—that it is really a woman's job."

"You mean you want me to help clear the place up a bit?"

"Precisely." He heaved a sigh of relief. "Poor Helena was never very orderly in her habits; and Leonora tells me that no modern domestic would stay for very long with the house as it is now. It is a most inconvenient request I know, but as a member of the family—" Somewhat brutally, with painful memories of sorting my own mother's effects after her death, I refused. It would mean days in that dreary house by the estuary, closeted with Austin who had been shell-shocked, whom I scarcely knew, and who was obviously most peculiar. Mr Galvain was rueful.

"I thought that you might feel that way," he said. "It is not your business, of course, and I realise that poor Austin can hardly have made a good impression upon you."

I asked why neither of Austin's sisters could go, and he explained again that Leonora was going to Paris for the spring shows, and that Melissa, he understood, had just been commissioned to decorate the state-rooms of S.S. "Megantic," and that in addition her family was home for the school holidays. I remained unimpressed. It seemed to me that if it was really all that urgent to clear up Greenbarns one or other of them might have managed it. "We must make other arrangements," said my host with a sigh.

We said good-bye then, after a few minutes of awkward conversation about trifles. I told myself that I had married Henry and not his relations, but I felt I had been ungracious.

In the end I went. Norrie wrote me a charming letter, full of apologies for not being able to go to Wiston herself, and Austin wrote too, asking me to come. Henry was at sea, and I really had no excuse for refusing. Besides, it is always flattering when people ask you to help them.

[II]

Austin met me at Chichester in his car, which was small and old and painted a bright blue, so that when he sat in it he looked like an overgrown baby in a bath. Remembering our former meeting I felt nervous at first that he should drive me, but to my surprise he was both careful and competent. He was brushed and tidy too this time and even looked a little less fat. He seemed very pleased to see me.

"You can't think how grateful I am to you, Susan," he said as he took my suitcase from the car. "I couldn't possibly deal with all this alone. Come in now and get warm." He put down his burden in the hall. "I think I'll leave this to Mrs Jilks," he said. "It's rather heavy. My heart, you know."

The house was more comfortable than I had dared to hope. Norrie had engaged "a good sensible woman" as advocated by Mr Galvain, and she seemed to be living up to the description. The brass knocker on the front door shone brightly and the step was white; the floor of the little hall was almost dangerously polished, and the whole place smelt faintly of beeswax and turpentine.

A fire burnt in the sitting-room, for the April evenings were still raw so near the sea, and tea was set ready on a low table.

"We thought you'd be cold after the journey," said Austin in his pleasant uncertain voice. "Ah, there you are my beauties!" He went on his knees over the basket of pugs who were sleeping by the fire, and they woke up, squealing and wriggling with joy and reaching out long crimson tongues to lick his face and hands. Pluto the parrot was roused by the commotion.

"Dirty little brutes!" he said viciously. "Dirty little brutes! Take them out of my clean drawing-room." He cracked a sunflower seed and nonchalantly tossed the husk on to the floor. "Dirty little brutes!" he repeated, and selected another seed from his jar.

Austin was patting the dogs and addressing them as "darling" and "sweetheart."

"Aren't they beautiful?" he asked me, his large face glowing in a grotesque parody of maternal pride. "Aren't they lovely? Did you ever see anything like them before?" I could truthfully answer that I had not.

"They'll come to you in a little while," he said consolingly, "but it takes them time to make friends. Actually—they don't like women, you know. They were much worse with Mrs Jilks. Come along, Dodie, now! Come on, Lela! Come on, Betty! Talk to the lady."

But the three pugs crouched in their basket gazing at me with pop-eyed apprehension, and no blandishments could bring them out. The one called Dodie, whose fat black back was a mass of ugly white scars, seemed particularly frightened, and every time I moved she gave a low, long growl.

"They'll get used to you in time," Austin assured me apologetically. He told me all their history, their ages and the prizes they had won and the number and careers of their offspring. They were some of the best dogs in the country, he said with pride.

Mrs Jilks came in with the teapot and a cakestand. She was a kind, clean-looking woman, and her welcome made me feel as though my hour's journey from London had been in the nature of a polar expedition. Pluto, who seemed to have a gift for the appropriate remark, immediately informed us in the most cajoling voice that what we wanted was a nice cup of tea. Austin clapped the cover over the cage promptly. "That bird!" he said crossly. "He gets on my nerves, you know, imitating poor mother like that."

"A nice cup of tea," murmured Pluto defiantly, and banged his beak on the wires of the cage. Austin removed him to the hall.

A nice cup of tea it certainly was, and now the sitting-room looked cosy and warm, though it was not quite my idea of what a sitting-room should be like. The walls were covered with pictures, photographs for the most part, and sentimental oil paintings of girls with doves, and impossible boats sailing into crimson sunsets. There was a cabinet full of shell and bead ornaments and purposeless curiosities including the ostrich-egg pincushion, and a gilded stand containing pots of ferns.

There was a large mahogany bureau with a book-case top in which were imprisoned in incongruous fellowship old medical books, odd copies of the English poets with the unreadable look of school prizes, and bound volumes of *Punch*. There was a grand piano which served as a display shelf for more photographs and pots of ferns, and a Turkey carpet at once garish and shabby. On the credit side were several comfortable armchairs with chintz covers, a radiogram, and a pair of exquisite Wedgwood urns which went with nothing else in the room.

It was a woman's room, except for the bookcase which was obviously a relic; and Austin's pipe and tobacco jar—tucked into a set of spindly shelves in company with a small china lady and an Indian brass box from Birmingham . . . did nothing to make it more masculine. Indeed, Austin, pouring out tea and talking in his light soft voice about his pugs, seemed himself to be slightly feminine. He had hands like a woman's, smooth and rather small, and he used them as he talked.

It was soon very obvious that the room had been tidy when we first came in, not because of Austin, but because of Mrs Jilks. Austin threw cushions off his chair, sat on the tea-cosy, scraped mud from his heels on to the brass fender, and strewed himself and the hearthrug with crumbs because he gesticulated with muffins and slices of cake. To my horrified amusement he ate such a tea as, regularly consumed, would have fattened the leanest. Buttered muffins and cream horns, bought he said when he met me in Chichester, vanished at speed, followed by two slices of rich and heavy plum cake and washed down by several cups of tea with cream and sugar.

"My doctor," he remarked finally, wiping his finger on a doubtful handkerchief, "has recommended me to eat plenty of nourishing food. A touch of gas in the last war, you know . . . affected my lungs slightly." He coughed twice as a proof of genuineness, lighted my cigarette and began to fill his pipe, scattering tobacco as he did so.

Comfortably drowsy from my journey and the heat of the fire I sat back in my chair. A shaft of sunlight fell smokily across the room and lay on the basket of pugs, now snoring gently. Dodie's back shone in a network of white weals. "What a pity that dog of yours is marked like that!" I remarked idly. "I suppose she got into some wire. It must have spoilt her for show."

Austin paused in the act of striking a match. "She's too old anyway," he said hastily, and his face assumed a curious shut expression. I asked him how he found Mrs Jilks.

"Unsympathetic." He sighed. "She has always been very strong herself, you know, and she hardly understands ill-health."

I said I had not realised that he was such an invalid, and he smiled bravely.

"One carries on. Poor Mother's death was a terrible shock to me . . . a terrible shock." He got up with a sudden heave. "I have some photographs of her here," he said almost shyly. "Perhaps you would like to look at them. She was very pretty," he added tenderly.

Pretty she can never have been, but she must have been very charming. Looking at the yellowing likenesses I began to understand why Mr Galvain had been so romantically attached to her in the old days. In the first picture, a head and shoulders portrait, the dark hair was piled high in curls and she was clothed to the chin in some stiff striped material. Her head was tilted stiffly against the lifted hand; her forehead was broad, and the melancholy of the eyes was belied by a smile, an amused and merry smile that was almost a grin.

"Before she married Father," Austin said significantly. "She told me once that she used to have dimples, but I never remember her like that. I remember this though."

It came from the piano and was framed in beaten silver. Young Mrs Prioleau sat on a high chair with two children at her knees and a third in her arms. The shining dark hair was brushed in wings from her face and she wore a white blouse and a wide dark skirt. Behind the group stood the doctor, bearded and solemn, with a hand laid on her shoulder. He seemed to me to have a slight look of Henry.

"That's me." Austin laid a pudgy finger on the figure of the small boy, a round-faced solemn child with his mother's beautiful eyes. "It was a green velvet suit and I was very proud of it. And that's Norrie, of course, and the baby's Mellie. We're both staring because the photographer told us to look at the camera hard and we should see a canary fly out." Mrs Prioleau was staring too out of mournful eyes, and there were shadows under the high cheek-bones. Mr Galvain had said that she was like a flame when she was young and that life had quenched her. When this picture was taken the quenching process must have begun. Her shoulders sagged wearily, and her head was inclined forward as though she had no interest to hold it up. She looked both sad and vacant.

"I like this one better," said Austin, "I made her have it taken last year, so that I could . . . so that I should have . . ." He swallowed as he handed me the big picture from the mantelpiece.

It was more than a mere likeness, this. It was a portrait, and the camera seemed, as happens perhaps once in a thousand times, to have caught the very essence of the sitter. Here was the dead mask I had seen before, but alive and smiling. The printing was soft so that the dark hair and the dark stuff of the dress melted into the background. The wide brow was still smooth, and under the heavy eyebrows the big eyes glowed. Dark lines ran from the nostrils to the corners of the mouth, and the jaw was heavy. Life had not quenched the flame in her after all, though it had been overlaid and smothered perhaps for a long time. Personality glowed in every line and contour of her face with a strange secretive brilliance. From the dark confines of her frame the late Mrs Prioleau confronted my gaze with a smile that was sinister and a little mad.

"Have you any other pictures of your father?" I asked, hardly knowing what remark to make.

"No." Austin answered abruptly. He waved his pipe round the pictures on the walls. "Mother did all these," he said, "when she was young. She wanted to be an artist, you know. She painted beautifully."

I looked once more at the array of pictures. They were unpleasantly emotional in conception, but the execution was good with a sureness of touch that removed them far beyond the amateur category.

"She was clever," I said.

"She was wonderful," Austin agreed fervently. He reminded me of a young man talking of his sweetheart. "She was a genius spoilt. Father never appreciated her I'm afraid." I asked him were there any photographs of Henry, but he told me no, and showed me one of himself instead in a lieutenant's uniform. He had been surprisingly handsome in those days. "You'd never think it, would you?" He shook his head as he put down the picture.

"Mother," he said, "never wanted Mellie and Henry, and she never liked them. She told me so."

With this surprising remark he leaned back again in his chair, with the appearance of settling down for a long talk; but unfortunately for my curiosity Mrs Jilks chose this moment to fetch the tea tray.

"The puppies' supper!" Austin's voice was shrill with dismay. "It's nearly half-an-hour late. I must go at once." Panting with anxiety he lumbered away and the pugs rose from the basket and followed him yapping.

At the door he turned. "My mouth-organ! I'd quite forgotten it! Excuse me, Susan." He came back to the couch and began rummaging among the cushions.

"Your pocket, Mr Prioleau," Mrs Jilks suggested.

"Ah!" He produced it triumphantly. "I always play to them when they're having supper," he explained. "They seem to like it."

He ambled away again followed by the pugs, their yapping mingled now with the strains of the "Old Hundredth."

"Goes through your head, doesn't it?" the housekeeper remarked sympathetically. "But there, I suppose it's a nice hobby for him if he likes them."

[III]

Mrs Jilks had done her best for my room, but it remained discouraging, the guest room of those who never had guests. It was filled with a large unfriendly brass bedstead and a gravy-coloured suite comprising wardrobe, dressing-table, washstand, and two chairs. Both carpet and wall-paper were old-fashioned and rather unpleasant in design, and they looked as though they might have been taken over from the previous tenant of the house. On the wall were three yellowing photographs of hirsute undergraduate groups, and more pictures, the less successful ones apparently, of girls and sunsets. There were crochet mats and hair-tidies on every available flat surface, and the mantelpiece was adorned with a bunch of very old paper roses in a sage green vase. A text, coyly surrounded by pansies, hung over the bed. It looked as though everything that should have been sent to a rummage sale had been poked away in this room and forgotten.

Round the window and on the ceiling were patches of damp, and the fire had done little to make the place more welcoming. The heat went smokily up the chimney and the air was chilly and smelt of disuse. Outside the evening sun still shone and a thrush whistled, but the window faced north and no brightness came through it to lighten the gloom. Mrs Jilks sniffed disgustedly.

"Three o'clock I lighted this fire, and no more heat out of it than that! I said to myself, 'that room's not been used for goodness knows how long, and the weather so cold for the time of year, and Mrs Prioleau coming all the way from London and driving out in that car with no proper hood to it!' Well, as I said to Mr Prioleau, we must all help each other, mustn't we? And I've got my own hot-water bottle in the bed, and the late Mrs Prioleau's too, and all the blankets have been in front of the fire. But I couldn't clear out the drawers, so I hope you haven't brought much with you."

Dramatically Mrs Jilks flung open the door of the wardrobe on a packed mass of garments and slammed it again. A drowsy clothes-moth fluttered out and she snatched furiously at it.

"That's what it's like, Mrs Prioleau! There'll be moths everywhere the first warm spell, you may depend on that. I spoke to Mr Prioleau about it because I have a nice coat of my own. . . . Four pound ten I paid for it in a sale at Barker's when Mr Jilks was alive. Lovely stuff it is! . . . but he said you were going to see about it. It'll take you all your time."

A little ruefully I agreed that I had come down to help Mr Prioleau look through Mrs Prioleau's things. "Humph!" said Mrs Jilks in ominous tones. "The mess here—well, you wouldn't believe it."

She checked herself and added that of course she shouldn't be talking like this to me, but she must say she would never have kept her house in such a state. Asking for trouble it was.

While she mended the fire and turned down the bed and brought me hot water she talked incessantly. She shouldn't say it, she knew, but she thought I would notice a difference in the house. That Mary had left the kitchen filthy, and 'the woman' was not much better. Well, poor Mr Prioleau was more comfortable now, she was sure of that, and happier in his mind too, poor fellow. It had been a dreadful shock, she was sure, but he was very good really and never said a word to her.

"You knew Mr Prioleau's mother well?" she asked me hopefully, and her face fell when I said that I had never met her.

"No more did I, of course, not being local, but she'd lived here a long time. She was very well known in the place."

Mrs Jilks swept the hearth with care. "I hope you have everything you want, Mrs Prioleau," she said. I answered that I had, and she withdrew reluctantly, leaving me with the impression that she knew a great deal, mostly discreditable, about my late mother-in-law.

I unpacked my night things, hung my coat and hat on a hook behind the door, and lay down on the bed with a book. The spring weather and the strong sea air had tired me, and I dozed off almost at once.

I was wakened with a start to hear a gust of raucous laughter, and two voices wishing each other good-morning over and over again. For a sleepy moment of horror I thought that Austin must be insane, and then I remembered Pluto. My room was over the hall and the deadening was bad, for I was spared no detail of his performance. His repertory included, among other items, a life-like imitation of courting cats, and he worked away at his effects like a fiddler practising for tone, making two or three sounds over and over again, and then two or three more, and pausing as it seemed, to judge the quality of his performance. Finally he appeared satisfied and began running through a dialogue piece.

"Austin!" he called. "Austin darling, where are you? . . . Yes, Mother, I'm coming. . . . Austin darling, where are my spectacles? Austin darling, find me my book, please. . . . A nice cup of tea! A nice cup of tea! What you want, my dear, is a nice cup of tea."

Pluto paused to rattle his bill on the bars of his cage, or so I judged from the faint metallic sounds that reached me. Then he began in a venomous voice: "I'll write that woman a letter. Such a letter! *Such* a letter!" He repeated the words on a crescendo of relish, and chuckled so that I almost felt uncomfortable to hear him. I remembered Cousin Liza and Uncle Septimus White at the funeral, and Austin's unhappy silence, and the way Mr Galvain had looked at him.

"Such a letter!" cried the horrible bird again with a hoot of joy. Then I heard steps. A door opened and shut again. Silence fell. I could picture Pluto brooding on his perch in the twilight of the green baize cover.

[IV]

The late Mrs Prioleau had been every whit as untidy as Austin, and it seemed as though in all her sixty-five years she had never got rid of anything. The congested wardrobe in my bedroom was only a sample of what awaited me in every room in the house, and it was not surprising that her daughters should have excused themselves from the arduous and unpleasant task of sorting her possessions.

"She threw away some things when we came from London," Austin said, "but I think most of it came down here in the drawers and things. . . ." And in the drawers it had apparently remained, as well as in all the cupboards and wardrobes, and in the assorted trunks and boxes which lay under a shroud of dust on the attic floor. I hardly knew where to begin.

Austin flapped about in the midst of the muddle, saying how thankful he was to have help, and adding to the confusion by knocking down and trampling upon everything within reach. He was entirely helpless, and indeed, by the time we had emptied out the contents of his mother's bedroom I began to feel helpless myself. It seemed incredible that any woman, even in a long lifetime, could have amassed so many clothes and oddments or accumulated so much rubbish. Good jewellery, scraps of paper, odd stockings, books, letters, underclothing, a half-smoked cigarette and a small pot of paste turned up in the first drawer we opened, while the contents of the second included a shoe, two gas accounts, garden secateurs and a Mason fruit plate.

"And we hunted the house for those secateurs!" Austin said. "Susan, it *is* good of you to be helping me like this!" I opened the third drawer on a tangle of ostrich feathers and bits of ribbon. I was beginning to agree with him.

Rapidly we reached the stage when every article seemed of its own accord to remove itself as soon as it was bestowed on the appropriate pile, and Austin's efforts did nothing to improve matters. I sent him to get dust-sheets from Mrs Jilks, and we spread them out and sorted into them, putting the hopeless rubbish on one side.

"You're so competent, Susan, so competent," Austin said, tripping over a shoe. "You know, all this stuff . . . well you know, I never should have thought. . ." He sat down heavily on the bed, and a pile of underwear slid to the floor.

I got rid of him by sending him to find out what was in the boxroom, and he returned with the glad news that most of the boxes contained nothing worse than odd rolls of wall-paper and linoleum, and medical books which had belonged to his father. He brought an old-fashioned hatbox down with him and the information that there was also a small trunk of clothes which could not well be handled by an asthmatic like himself. We fetched it down together. It was quite light. "I have to be a little careful of my heart, you see," he explained apologetically.

Clothes are revealing things. Colour, size, shape, style, the kneeing of trousers or the stretch of skirts, sketch the mental and physical peculiarities of the wearer with pitiless clarity. Not only had the late Mrs Prioleau been extremely untidy; she had also, on occasion, worn remarkably striking and theatrical clothes. She had three long gowns of fine wool in saffron yellow, purple and royal blue, with a Celtic look about them, and another in crimson velvet, and she had a rather beautiful scarlet cloak faced with silk to match, and a black one lined with jade green. Austin told me that she sometimes put on one or other of the dresses in the evenings, and that a cloak had been her usual wear on her rare excursions into Chichester. "People used to stare rather," he said, "but I think she liked that. She looked very striking certainly. I think there was some rumour that she was a Russian princess. She liked that too." He gave a little giggle. "I never felt I fitted into the picture."

Mrs Prioleau's everyday garments were in sordid contrast to her finery, a collection of dirty dilapidated old jumpers and skirts and cheap summer frocks. Their frowsy smell and tossed appearance were unpleasantly suggestive of an old clothes shop and I hated touching them. The obvious thing was to have handed the whole horrible collection over to a dealer, but some of the jumpers had quite good brooches stuck in them, and there were bills and private letters in the pockets of coats, and small pieces of china and old silver tucked away all over the place. We had to go separately through everything.

Austin collected all the scraps of paper with a strange careful furtiveness, as though he were afraid of my reading them. "We'll burn these," he said. "They don't need to be kept." He put them all together into the wastepaper-basket, and then emptied them into the grate and set a match to them.

Finally we opened the boxes from the attic. A smell of lavender came from them, and the contents were folded in tissue paper. One by one I lifted out half a dozen dresses, carefully folded, with sprays of lavender and sweet-woodruff lying among the time-yellowed wrappings.

"Well, I'll be blowed!" said Austin. "She must have had those when she was first married!"

They were the kind of clothes I had never seen except in pictures, clothes in the fashions of the very early nineteen-hundreds, just after the period of the shirtwaist and the boater hat. There were three hats in the hatbox, a large picture hat of supple straw trimmed with blue ostrich feathers, a tiny "Dolly Varden" in pink moiré with flowers under the brim, and a winter hat of black velvet with great black wings sweeping back across the sides of the crown.

The dresses in the trunk went with the hats, and there were several evening ones besides. Prolonged storage had taken some of the freshness from the frilled organdie with the green bows, and the brocade evening gown, a low-cut affair with a long train, was cutting slightly at the seams. But the blue woollen day dress with the squirrel trimmings and the gay little pairs of slippers looked as though they had just come from the shop, and there were six pairs of long kid gloves still folded in the original paper. Austin looked at the brocade evening-dress, turned it over, examined it, felt the material between finger and thumb.

"Good Lord, Susan! Why, I remember this. It must have been when we were *very* small, Norrie and I. One evening Mother came in to tuck us up and she was wearing this, and she smelt of flowers and I thought she was lovely. Then she said she was going off with the fairy prince, and we both howled because we wanted to go too. In the end she laughed and said she'd take me with her, but she told Norrie that she was Father's little girl or something, and Norrie was furious. I wonder if she remembers. She had a candle in her hand and it shone on her, so that she looked as if she was made of gold. Norrie said she was going to have a dress like that when she was grown up, but I couldn't have one because I was a boy. I was awfully disappointed. Funny the things you remember!"

He shook his head over the other clothes and said he did not recollect seeing them. "I don't think she ever wore them, but then of course you don't remember everything when you're a kid, or she may have worn them when we weren't there, or something."

"They haven't been worn very much."

"Well, they don't look much like the Kennington Road, do they? Of course, I don't know, but they look to me rather too smart. I think she must have got them for a holiday or something, and then they didn't go. Poor mother! She always liked nice clothes, and Father never cared tuppence."

I looked again at the dresses, lying in a tangle of colours over the dingy rubbish that cluttered the bed. They were handmade, even to the seams, sewn with tiny neat stitches and beautifully finished.

"I believe Mother used to sew very nicely," Austin remarked. "Aunt Catherine once told me . . . before the quarrel of course. I wonder if she made them, or something. . . ."

We had come to the end of his mother's wardrobe, and I asked him what he thought we should do with everything. He looked vague and worried and said he didn't know. What did you do with people's clothes when they were dead? I answered that I supposed you gave them away or sold them. After lengthy consideration he said perhaps we might offer Mrs Jilks something, or Norrie and Melissa. Well, perhaps not. They probably had enough clothes already.

"And what shall we do with the rest? What about a dealer?"

"I think we'd better put it all away again," Austin said hopefully. "It doesn't take very much room."

"Yes, but what about moths? And supposing you want to move?" His face took on a mulish expression.

"I don't want to move, and I don't mind the moths."

This was not especially helpful in view of what Mr Galvain had said, not to mention Mrs Jilks with her lovely coat. I protested gently. Austin waved his hands. His mouth opened and shut like a fish's and he looked quite upset.

"You know, it's horrible, Susan . . . all her clothes. Getting rid of them like that. The only things I have to remind me of her." I returned to the charge, feeling by now slightly exasperated. "Why not send them to some charity that distributes clothing? They'd be glad to have them, you know." It was ridiculous that all this jumble should be returned to collect more moths in the drawers we had just taken it from. I said so.

"Mother wouldn't like other people wearing her clothes," Austin answered stubbornly. "You know, Susan, she always took such a pride in them." I bit back the answer that most of them were not objects of pride.

I told him that I sympathised with him very much and that he must feel it all horribly, and then with what seemed a flash of inspiration I suggested that we might offer the dresses from the little trunk and the hats that went with them to the costume section of the London Museum. "No one would wear them there, and they would be set out on stands in glass cases for people to admire them."

"I don't know," murmured Austin vaguely, sitting down within an inch of the largest hat. "What about burning them? Don't you think it would be quite a good idea? We could pour some paraffin on them or something, and burn them at the bottom of the garden."

"Well, I suppose we *could*. But have you ever tried burning tweed coats, or brogues, or fur trimmings?"

"No. But I'm sure we could manage."

I had a fairly good idea who would do the managing, and said that it would be difficult. Austin replied drearily that he supposed so, and sat back on the bed with a discouraged expression. I went on sorting, picking out warm woollens and tweeds and folding them, in the hopes that in time my brother-in-law would see reason and agree to give them to people who could use them.

Austin remained silent, incongruously surrounded with evening dresses and elaborate hats, staring at nothing. He looked somehow lost and pathetic in spite of his bulk. Temporarily matters seemed to have reached a deadlock. Rashly I mentioned that the *Times* was always full of requests for old clothes for people in poor parishes. "We can send them just as they are," I explained, "sewn up in the sheet with rope round them. I'll do it if you like, and you needn't have anything to do with it." I would have promised anything to get some of the mess cleared up. Austin said nothing.

To my horror I saw that his large pansy-blue eyes were filling with tears. "Oh, Susan," he said. "You can't imagine how I miss her!" His face was working. He gave a great gulp.

"She was everything to me—everything. I don't know what to do now she's gone. She used to do everything—arrange everything—except over the dogs. . . . She didn't like them, you know—and now she's gone."

"Austin! Stop it! Be quiet!" The scene was becoming unpleasantly like the previous one on the day of the funeral when I had seen him for the first time in that same room, weeping over the open coffin. And yet I had a curious feeling that this time his emotion was less genuine, that he was working himself up deliberately.

"All her clothes . . . her things!" he lamented incoherently. "Oh Mother, Mother! Come back! Come back!"

He flung himself on the bed in a passion of crying. He shook horribly, like a jelly, with his coat seams straining on his shoulders; the knobs on the bedstead rattled in time to his sobs. It was pathetic and funny and disgusting all at once.

"Austin!" I implored him. "Be quiet! Mrs Jilks will hear you." But it was no good. Even genuine grief, carried to excess, is exasperating, and this dramatic ululation made me suddenly quite furious. It was so silly and so noisy that all my pity left me.

Years before I had seen a case of hysterics dealt with by an old-fashioned doctor with a jug of cold water. I seized the bedroom jug which happened to be full, and held it over his head.

"Austin!" I shouted loudly in his ear. "If you don't stop making that noise *this instant* I shall pour water over you. Do you hear? I mean it." Renewed bawlings answered my threat. Carefully clearing the bed of clothes I tipped the water over his head and shoulders.

He rose to his feet dripping and gasping, with an expression of rage on his streaming face. My own rage was satisfied, and I remembered with horror that he was shell-shocked, unstable, four times as large as myself. I backed towards the door, menacing him with the half empty jug and hoping wildly that Mrs Jilks was within earshot. "I'll throw the rest over you," I threatened. "I've got some more." I felt very frightened.

But Austin only gasped and shook his head. There is a good deal of cold water in a bedroom jug. "Sorry, Susan," he said meekly, and sat back on the soaking bed. The last I saw of him as I left the room he was mopping himself thoughtfully on a white flannel nightdress and sniffing.

[V]

I hate scenes. I was not brought up to them and they upset me thoroughly. I sat in the sitting-room and felt my knees weak and my head aching. I had the disagreeable feeling that I had bungled things badly, and I had no idea what I should say to Austin when next I saw him, if indeed I saw him at all. It was all very unpleasant.

Mrs Jilks appeared within the minute. She must have been listening, and indeed she had hardly needed to strain her ears.

"Really good coffee, Mrs Prioleau," she said, placing a tray before me and pouring out my cup. "It'll do you good. And here are some little cakes I just popped in the oven, because as I said to myself, when people are working hard—and it *is* working hard looking over all that ru—stuff . . . they're bound to be hungry, and there's nothing like a nice cup of coffee to cheer you up when you're feeling low! Drink it up, dear. You're looking very tired."

I was touched by her solicitude, until she volunteered to run upstairs and take a cup to Mr Prioleau. In a fatuous effort to preserve the decencies I answered that he was very busy and I would take him up a cup myself later on.

Mrs Jilks nodded sympathetically. She had all the appearance of settling down for a chat, and I realised that the tray of coffee had been in the nature of a bribe.

"Poor Mr Prioleau!" she remarked. "Frets after his mother terribly! He gets these turns sometimes if anything upsets him. Other times he's as bright as a button, cracking jokes and singing round the place, and playing with those funny little dogs of his. Your coffee all right, Mrs Prioleau? Mr Jilks always liked it like that."

"What you want, my dear," remarked the parrot suddenly, roused by the chinking of china, "is a good cup of tea."

"There now!" Mrs Jilks exclaimed. "If he isn't just like a human. Mr Prioleau doesn't like him though. Reminds him of his poor mother, I expect."

"She ought to be written to," Pluto interposed with his most sinister chuckle.

"Nasty things, parrots! Gives you the creeps, this one does. He knows a sight more than he should about this house too, if you ask me." She put the green cover over the cage and Pluto became silent.

"Mr Prioleau wouldn't have anything happen to that parrot all the same—not for a hundred pounds. He told me so. His mother was simply set on it."

Mrs Jilks filled my empty cup and made a show of dusting the mantelpiece ornaments. I did not want her to talk to me, but she was determined, and I was feeling too upset to do anything about it.

"From all accounts," she remarked mysteriously, "Mrs Prioleau seems to have been a queer old lady."

I answered "Oh!" in my most discouraging voice.

"And Mr Prioleau such a nice gentleman," Mrs Jilks continued, after waiting vainly for the question that was not put.

"Yes. Yes, he is nice. You like it here then?"

"Yes. But from what I hear I shouldn't have liked it so well when she was alive. My husband's brother-in-law lives down here . . . well really I came here through him when Mr Jilks passed away . . . and he tells me things. He said he wouldn't have advised me to come if the old lady was still alive, but her being dead made it different. Well, poor thing, she *is* dead now, so I suppose I ought not to talk like that, but they do say. . . ." Her voice sank to a half-whisper. "They do say she *made mischief*. There was a girl killed herself—hanged in her mother's scullery—and they do say . . . well, she'd been working here, and no one else could have known she was in trouble."

The housekeeper pronounced the words with relish. She was like a famished woman in front of a juicy steak, a drunkard in sight of a full bottle. She was longing to tell me all about what "They" said of my late mother-in-law. "That Pluto," she said. "Always going on about writing letters. It seems queer, don't you think so, Mrs Prioleau?"

But I felt that this one-sided conversation had gone on for long enough. The woman was a gossip, a dangerous gossip, and it was unseemly for me to scavenge round the memory of Henry's mother. I thanked her for my coffee, and said that I was going out for some air. She sighed audibly as she removed the tray.

I went upstairs for my coat. The door of Mrs Prioleau's bedroom stood open, and there was no sign of Austin. I felt grateful for the respite. The air of the house seemed heavy, heavy with the smell of old clothes and old bitter grudges and dirty little whisperings in stuffy corners. Outside the sun shone. I went into the garden.

Weeds were beginning to sprout in the beds and the grass on the little lawn was over-long, but obviously, until the last few weeks, it had been well kept for a number of years. Under the windows wallflowers were in bloom, and clumps of daffodils grew everywhere. There were beds of roses, still unpruned, with long stout shoots showing the first leaves of the year. There was a small rock-garden, with patches of tiny strange plants just breaking in the pockets of the earth and a pool with gold-fish. A row of espaliers hid the vegetable garden and an old brick wall ran round the whole, sheltering it from the cold sea wind. The sight of Mrs Prioleau's garden made me feel almost kindly disposed to her again.

Quietly, still not too anxious to encounter Austin, I slipped out of the gate, and turned right to the village half a mile away. I wanted to get some cigarettes, and to enquire about 'buses to Chichester, in case I should find that my host was quarrelling with me.

It was a lovely day, cold and clear, filling the flat landscape with changing subtle colours, and for the first time I realised that the place had its fascinations, even though it was a queer isolated spot for an old lady to choose to live.

As I walked I thought of the incredible medley of garments still lying scattered over her bedroom. Long ago when she had collected her bright pretty clothes and frivolous hats, she was certainly not thinking of the Sussex marshes. She was thinking of Paris, the Riviera, Venice with the Fairy Prince. Those boxes from the attic held something more than costumes of a dead fashion. They were the silent record of disappointment, perhaps tragedy. It was a good idea for a short story. I began to plan it.

I was interrupted by a breathless voice calling my name. Turning round I saw a small stout lady, curiously attired and breathless from hurrying.

"Mrs Prioleau!" she called. "Mrs Prioleau!" I stopped. "You *are* Mrs Prioleau? Young Mrs Prioleau, I mean? I'm Lucy Trip. I saw you coming out of the gate at Greenbarns . . . I live just down the lane—and Mrs Jilks had told me you were coming, so I thought it must be you. I'm going to the village. Are you?"

I replied that I was going to buy cigarettes.

"Nasty things," observed Miss Trip amiably. "They cause the juices of the stomach to ferment. I heard you were coming only yesterday. It's a gossipy place, you know, but excellent for the Vibrations. Flat country like this presents no obstacle." She waved a podgy hand. "Water is an excellent conductor too. You live in London?"

I answered that for the time being I had no settled home.

"Ah! Are you sensitive?" She looked up at me earnestly. "Yes, I can see you are. You probably find the place too strong for you." I replied that it seemed bracing, and that I supposed it was the sea air.

"Yes. That's what most people say. But they're wrong. It isn't the air. It's the Vibrations, and until you grow accustomed to them you feel them. But they do you good. Look at me now. Why, if anything I'm too fat, but when I came down here two years ago I was a wreck. Positively. Insomnia, indigestion! And thin! Terrible! I'd been in London, and it didn't suit me . . . not even on the top storey. All those houses interfere with the Vibrations, and I'm extremely sensitive. I require them, you know. So I moved and came here, and I've never regretted it. Never."

I said that that was very fortunate.

"Mrs Prioleau," she spoke accusingly, "Mr Prioleau's mother, I mean . . . showed no reactions to the Vibrations. In fact the only time I saw her she told me she didn't believe in them." Miss Trip sighed. "If I may say so to you without offence, I am afraid your late mother-in-law was something of a crank."

We reached the shop. I bought cigarettes furtively and told Miss Trip that they were for Austin. She replied that she believed he always smoked a pipe. Anyway he was, she feared, too stout to be sensitive to the Vibrations.

"Well, perhaps he's lucky. He could probably live in London and not mind." Miss Trip agreed rather sadly that this might be so.

She was an entertaining little creature, since I would probably never see her for long enough to be bored with the Higher Life. She walked back with me along the road to Greenbarns, talking all the time. She lived alone, she told me, and she talked in the overwhelming manner of lonely people, taking her breath in gulps like a swimmer doing the crawl . . . From Vibrations we passed to the Danger of Milk, and thence, by stages, to the transmigration of souls. Like most people who hold this belief, her previous lives had been lived among the famous of the earth. She had been in turn Helen of Troy, Heloise, Ann Boleyn, and lastly, because she had died violently, she had returned to earth as Charles II's favourite spaniel.

"He loved me," she explained, "and I adored him. But of course animals feel these things so acutely. They have no outlet, as we have." A sudden thought seemed to strike her, and she stopped dead in the road, clutching my arm impressively.

"They tortured dogs at Greenbarns," she said in a husky voice. I saw again the fat black back with the silvery weals.

"Nonsense," I said feebly. "You must be mistaken."

But Miss Trip was firm. She had heard them screaming twice when Mr Prioleau was out, and she had told the police about it and they had gone to see Mr Prioleau. Mr Prioleau said that one of the dogs had torn its back on some wire, and it cried when it was being dressed. But she didn't believe it because she knew he was out at the time, and Mrs Prioleau had never liked the dogs and would not have done dressings on them under any circumstances.

It seemed impossible for me to escape from unpleasant reminiscences of my dead mother-in-law. Miss Trip, who was obviously a little crazy, was determined to tell me all about her from her own rather peculiar angle.

"You understand," she explained. "You feel the Vibrations. But Mrs Prioleau was an Earthbound Soul. She lived emotionally, sensually, without any care for the things of the spirit."

"She painted beautifully."

"Yes. But she never tried to live the Good Life. She ate what she liked. She did what she liked. And when I saw her with her son, his poor soul seemed to be eaten up by hers. When she is born again she will be an Earthbound Soul, tied to this world even more closely than before, and because she tortured defenceless things she herself will be defenceless."

We were outside the gate of Greenbarns by this time, and her voice had risen to such a pitch of prophetic strength that I was afraid Austin or Mrs Jilks might hear her. I said "yes, yes," and fumbled for the latch. Her parting shot was unexpected and embarrassing.

"Good-bye," she said, not without dignity. "I've so much enjoyed our little chat. I know you think I'm mad. Most people do. But what I have told you is perfectly true. Now that she has gone his soul may grow to its proper stature."

[VI]

When Austin and I met at lunch, he seemed to be quite recovered from his attack of grief, having apparently the ability, like many hysterical people, of forgetting all about a scene as soon as it is over. His shirt collar still looked slightly damp and his face a trifle puffy, and he eyed me a little furtively, as though he were trying to decide what I was thinking. But he ate and enjoyed a large luncheon, and talked to me as if we had both spent our morning in the most normal way possible.

He was going to a dog show in Chichester that afternoon, and he pressed me to go with him. He was showing Gay Laddie and Fairy Queen and Beauty of Sussex, and he was certain to win, and I could sit with him by the show table and see everything, and we would have tea afterwards in that nice little shop by the church that sold such good cakes. He made it sound quite alluring. But I once went to a dog show, and I know that it is certainly one of the noisiest entertainments in the world. When he added that he was sure I wouldn't mind nursing the dogs in the car I told him that I must stay behind and write a letter to Henry.

So Austin went to his dog show, and I finished tidying the horrible bedroom upstairs, and then sat in the sitting-room and wrote my letter. The bright day had broken in cold squalls of rain and I was glad of the fire that Mrs Jilks had lighted for me. The pugs that were not going to the show had been put away in some outhouse, and I banished Pluto to the dining-room with the cover over his cage. Mrs Jilks remained in the kitchen. I wrote my letter and read my library book and felt comfortable and at peace. She brought my tea in at four o'clock. She showed some wish to linger, but I entrenched myself behind the *Times*, which is a good-sized protection, and said "yes" and "no" to her remarks until she gave up trying to talk to me.

I was pouring out my first cup of tea when a car stopped wheezily in the lane, and I heard the latch of the gate lifted. Then came a ring at the door and a man's voice talking to Mrs Jilks. She told him that Mr Prioleau was at a dog show in Chichester, and I waited hopefully for him to depart. My book was a good one, and it was pleasant to be alone. Instead to my annoyance I heard the front door shut behind the stranger and his voice booming in the little hall.

"I know. I've just seen him there. I've come along to see Mrs Prioleau if she's in."

Mrs Jilks replied hospitably that I was just having tea and that she would bring another cup, and reluctantly I put down my book. It seemed a little hard that I should be obliged to entertain Austin's friends in his absence.

My visitor announced himself by a perfunctory knock on the sitting-room door and walked in before I could answer.

"Mrs Prioleau? I hope you don't mind my coming in like this. I'm Lorton, Mrs Prioleau's doctor, and I thought I'd like a few words with you. I met Austin in Chichester, and he told me he had you with him."

The doctor sat down, stretching out a pair of long legs in shabby trousers, and remarked that it was a disappointing afternoon after such a fine morning, and I filled his cup and wondered why on earth he had come to see me.

He was in no hurry to enlighten me either. He ate his tea, and smoked his pipe, which bubbled foully, and told me that he had been more than fifteen years in the district, and that the sea air kept everyone infernally healthy or killed 'em outright, and that it was a poor place for a doctor. But he wouldn't shift all the same. He liked the people, and he was a yachtsman and a bird watcher, and the place grew on you. He talked in a pleasant rattling way as if nothing were of any particular consequence, but his small clever eyes took stock of me while he spoke, and I knew that he had called for more than a cup of tea.

How did I like the place? he asked me, feeling his way. And had Austin given me a lot to do? He had said something about sorting things. Galvain's doing, Dr Lorton supposed. It was very good of me to come down and take so much trouble, and Austin said I had been such a help. He supposed I knew them all well?

A pause. I dislike anyone trying to pump me because it insults my intelligence, and I never knowingly yield to pumping. Dr Lorton gave me another searching look and made up his mind to direct attack.

"You're wondering what I've come for, aren't you, Mrs Prioleau? You're quite right. It wasn't my tea, though I've enjoyed it very much, thank you. I've come to discuss Austin with you. How do you find him?"

I asked him what he meant, though I thought I knew, for there was a twinkle in his eye.

"Mrs Prioleau. I don't know you, of course, and so I don't know how well you normally look. But I do know that you're looking dead tired now. Has Austin been behaving himself? He's pretty trying sometimes. Has he been making scenes?"

I told him about the jug of water and he roared with laughter.

"That's just what I've been wanting to do to him for years, only Helena would never have let me inside the house again if I had, and I promised the old man to keep an eye on them. He took me into partnership the year before he died, and he made me his executor. I brought them down here as a matter of fact. They moved to Rye after he died, and she got herself into rather a fix there! . . . I needn't go into it . . . so when this house fell empty Galvain and I persuaded her to settle here. She needed someone to keep her in hand."

Dr Lorton paused, wrinkling his brows. I got the impression that there were a whole lot of things, more or less unpleasant, that he could tell me about Henry's mother if he wanted to, and he was debating within himself how much he needed to say. I wondered why he should feel it necessary to say anything at all, now that she was dead and could get herself into no more fixes.

"Have you any influence with Austin?" he asked me suddenly. "He ought to leave the place, and he doesn't want to. Galvain says he will have just enough to hang on here after it's all been cleared up, but . . . he should go. Make a fresh start somewhere."

I was unsympathetic. It appeared to me that too much fuss was being made about the ridiculous Austin. I said that he seemed very comfortable, and he was probably as happy here as he would be anywhere. It seemed a pity to uproot him if it could be avoided.

"No, he ought to move." Dr Lorton spoke decidedly. "And he never will. He'll probably turn the place into a sort of shrine, and go on doing nothing, and getting fatter and fatter because he likes cream cakes and hates walking. And I shall have to prescribe for him when he gets fatty degeneration." He spoke with bitterness. "Yes, I know you think I'm unkind, but I know this family very well, Mrs Prioleau, and I *think* I know Austin. He's a hypochondriac, to be quite brutal, and his mother turned him into one. I'm not saying he's a healthy man, of course. He's too fat. But he has neither a bad heart nor asthma. He's a very nice fellow really, when you get past the nonsense—wouldn't hurt a fly. But he's bone idle, and his mother undermined him so thoroughly that now whenever anything shows signs of becoming unpleasant he avoids it by making a scene, like the one he treated you to this morning. He's a conundrum all right, and, if you will forgive my saying so, neither your husband nor his sisters have ever taken full responsibility. It was difficult, of course, because of Mrs Prioleau's attitude, but I feel very strongly now that something should be done."

Dr Lorton appeared to consider again. He picked up a sandwich and chewed it thoughtfully, and walked round the room, scratching a red and hairy ear. Finally he took a deep breath and sat down again.

"Mrs Prioleau, I will be frank with you. There are things that someone in this family ought to know, and as you are here, I am afraid it will have to be you. Galvain knows about it. In fact we discussed it together some time ago. But he's too cautious. Hates committing himself, like all lawyers, and would very probably disapprove strongly of my talking to you like this. I would rather talk to your husband, anyway, or to Mrs Campion, because it would require less explanation. But you are here and they are not. I say that Austin should leave this house and this neighbourhood and make a fresh start, and that is my considered opinion both as a medical man and as a man of the world."

I asked him why he was so emphatic. Austin's life was by no means an ideal one, but it was probably as good a life as he would make for himself anywhere, and Mrs Jilks appeared to like him and to make him very comfortable.

"Mrs Jilks? Oh, I'm not saying anything about her. She seems an excellent woman. But in the first place there's too much of Mrs Prioleau about this house, and in the second . . . Did Mrs Jilks say anything to you that struck you as at all curious?"

"Well, she dropped dark hints."

"Exactly. And you've heard that wretched parrot?"

"About writing the letter?"

"Yes. I've arranged to get rid of him by the way. The brute ought to have his neck wrung, but Austin won't hear of it. He's going to an old servant in London somewhere, or at least I hope he is. No accounting for tastes; she wrote and asked if she could have him if he was still alive and no one wanted him. Well, doesn't that remark about the letter suggest anything to you?"

It certainly did. It suggested to me that Henry's mother had been disagreeable and quarrelsome and that she had written objectionable letters to various people, among whom were undoubtedly Cousin Liza and the unpleasant Uncle Septimus White. There seemed to be no more to it than that, and I wondered more than ever why Dr Lorton was making such a fuss.

"Mrs Prioleau," he said, very seriously. "I am sorry to have to tell you all this, and to ask you to repeat at least some of it to your husband. Helena was once a very good friend of mine, and now she is dead and I would not speak of her like this, except that it concerns Austin. To be quite frank, in her later years your mother-in-law was a most unpleasant and dangerous woman. She fought with all her relations, though I'm afraid that is by no means an unheard-of thing, and she made mischief in whatever neighbourhood she was in.

"There was a plague of anonymous letters when they lived in Rye . . . the usual dirty little lies with just a hint of truth at the bottom . . . and two people at least were so bothered by them that they called in the police. I only got to know because she received some too, and showed them to Galvain . . . some silly rubbish about Austin being illegitimate, I think. Well, something in her manner when she showed them to him made Galvain suspicious, and he got an expert to compare them with her usual writing. Goodness knows why she did it . . . unless she found country life dull and wanted a little excitement . . . but anyway he was afraid of it being brought home to her. Fortunately the lease of the house there was nearly up, and she was tired of the place, and she fancied it didn't suit Austin. So he and I put our heads together, and got her down here. Mrs Campion was in New York at the time, and your husband was only a boy and Mrs Hillier has always refused to interest herself in the family in any way. We both tried talking to Austin, but he couldn't or wouldn't believe anything wrong about his mother. Galvain and I were the only people who were willing to be in any way responsible, and it seemed the best way out.

"That was five years ago, and so far as I know she was quite quiet until the last couple of months. Then I began to hear things. There was nothing that attached directly to her, but knowing her I had my suspicions. I tried speaking to Austin again, but it was absolutely hopeless. At the beginning of this year her maid left in a hurry . . . She was a local girl . . . very respectable family . . . and hanged herself in her mother's kitchen a week later . . . The usual thing. I did the autopsy. It turned out that she had received three letters which she had shown to no one and which had upset her very much. They couldn't be found, luckily, and I managed to keep them out of the inquest, but her mother was sure they were from Mrs Prioleau, and of course she's talked, or at least she's dropped hints. The whole neighbourhood knows by now who wrote those letters, and what was in them."

Dr Lorton shrugged his shoulders expressively. His kind face wore a look of disgust and regret.

"I hate telling you all this," he said, "but you see now what I mean about Austin being better out of the place. Besides, there's more to it than that. Austin adores those dogs of his and Helena adored Austin. Poor woman!

"Circumstances and her own temperament focused all her affection on him, and she was jealous of anything or anybody that attracted his attention from her. A month ago it was all over the village that she used to torture the dogs. There again I don't *know*. But I know Helena, and I think she would have been perfectly capable of anything where Austin was concerned. Besides the main point is that people here *believe* she did these things, and while Austin lives here—you see what I mean?"

"Yes, I see."

Dr Lorton was fidgeting about the room in the irritating way that some people fidget when they are thinking. He was talking now as much to himself as to me.

"It's a dreadful thing to have to say, but in my opinion her death was most fortunate. If she had lived another month she would have been in the courts. Of course I knew her heart was weak, that any sudden shock might kill her, but she might have lived for years. Death is not often so considerate."

"Why didn't you speak about this a long time ago?" I asked him. "The time to tell Henry and Norrie that their mother wrote anonymous letters and might be sent to prison was surely while she was alive to write them."

"No good." Dr Lorton began to refill his bubbly pipe. "When the trouble started in the first place Henry and Mrs Campion were both abroad as I said, and Mrs Hillier had no influence on her at all. There's no good in stirring up mud and worrying people to no purpose. The week before she died I actually got on to Galvain about the new business, and we were going to tell her children what was happening. When she went he had actually written to Henry asking if he could see him. Austin was no help at all, of course. None whatever. She had such complete control over him, except over those dogs, that no one could have made him act in any way contrary to her wishes. When I tried to talk to him he shut up like a clam, and when Galvain tried he took the line that the whole world was against his mother and he was her only protector. Oh, she ate him up all right. She adored him, of course, and he her, but it always seemed to me a thoroughly unhealthy relationship. They reminded me of a married couple where the wife runs the show and the husband walks behind saying 'yes, darling,' and paying the bills. Only Austin didn't even have to pay the bills. She did all that, and a fine mess she made of it, by the way.

"That's why Austin should leave the district. He has no standing here because he was always so obviously his mother's shadow. If people think of him at all, they think of him as mad or a chronic invalid or both, and all the rumours that circulated about her will attach themselves to him, and he will never have even a chance of being normal."

I said that I saw his point, and that I would do my best to influence Austin, though I was not very hopeful. I asked him what I should do about the clothes and to my relief he promised to see about them. Then he returned again to the subject of Austin.

"It was a terrible shock to him finding her dead in bed like that, and when I arrived he was beside himself with hysteria, and saying that he had killed her and that it was all his fault. In the end I had to tell him that if he went on saying it someone might believe him and send for the police. The way things were I didn't like it at all . . . not that I believed it for a moment, naturally.

"I never saw him over the funeral, because I had 'flu on me and a bad baby case at the same time, but I saw him a couple of days later and he was extraordinarily cheerful. I've seen him once or twice since, and he almost seems to me to have improved, to be standing on his own feet a little more. I think he feels free for the first time in his life. But when I suggested to him the other day that he might try to find something to do, he was back to his old tack . . . his health. Mother had always been the only one who understood him, and he was so lonely and miserable without her, and so on and so forth. Disgusting! She always stood between him and the world while she was alive, and now he's using her memory as a kind of umbrella. He didn't even sound genuine."

The clock struck five and Dr Lorton rose. "Well, I'd better be going. Thank you for my tea, Mrs Prioleau, and thank you for listening to me for so long."

I said it was good of him to take so much trouble. He shrugged his shoulders.

"Patient of mine, and I like him, in spite of all I have been saying. Besides I owe it to his father. He was a wonderful man. And poor Helena. Well, goodbye."

I saw him to the gate. The ugly pleasant sitting-room seemed suddenly to have lost all its pleasantness. Now that Dr Lorton had the matter of the clothes in hand I decided then and there that I would go back to London next morning.

[VII]

Austin returned from his dog show shortly after six, bringing with him a first prize, a highly commended, and a bottle of rather nasty sweet champagne on which we celebrated at dinner.

He was delighted with himself and chatted unceasingly like a small boy who has done something clever. My head spun in a jargon of "dome" and "brindling," "short-coupled" and "cobby," and he told me every detail of the afternoon, and what the judges had said, and how he could have sold Fairy Queen and Gay Laddie twenty times over for quite improbable sums. It appeared too that everyone whose opinion was worth having . . . excepting the judges . . . had been more than surprised that Gay Laddie had been placed so low in the puppy class, and old Miss Missenden, who had been for fifty years in the fancy, had given it as her opinion that he was worth a first, and she probably knew more about pugs than anyone in England. Still, these local affairs were always a toss-up, and anyway they were only practice. Gave you an idea how a dog showed. What really counted was the big shows. Gay Laddie should do pretty well later at Crufts . . .

might even get a championship eventually if he shaped as well as he seemed to be doing.

"He's a born show dog, Susan. Has all the tricks naturally. Some of them have, you know. You must come and see him win. I'll write to you nearer the time and we'll fix it up. I know you'll enjoy it."

There was something comic and rather engaging about Austin when he talked about his dogs. His face lit up with a wide rapturous smile, and he related the compliments which his dogs had received almost coyly, as though they had been paid to himself. The words would hardly come fast enough. He stammered more than ever and drew pictures on the table-cloth with a fork to show me what a perfect pug ought to look like. He was so natural and normal, so different from the miserable creature that he had been in the morning that I found myself for the first time really liking him. He was so obviously anxious to be liked and so delighted to have an attentive audience that it was painfully clear he had received little encouragement in the past. He fairly revelled in it, and his enthusiasm communicated itself to me so that I was quite sorry I had refused to go with him in the afternoon.

"It is so nice to have someone to talk to who is really interested," he said happily, helping himself a second time to treacle pudding. "It makes it all seem so much more worth doing. Poor mother always thought shows were too much excitement for me, and that they brought on my asthma. But I'm sure they don't do me any harm really, and I do enjoy them so much."

Mrs Jilks came and cleared away the pudding and put the fruit on the table. Peaches, and a bunch of golden-green hot-house grapes glowed in the dish before him.

"They were awfully expensive," he told me naively, "but I *do* love grapes, and this is a bit of an occasion."

Neatly he dismembered the bunch on to our respective plates, and refilled our glasses with the champagne. Now was the time, when he was so pleased with himself and me, to have broached the subject of his leaving Greenbarns. Instead, the demon of curiosity entered into me, and when he started again to talk about his dogs, I asked him point blank what his mother had done to Dodie. His face clouded so obviously that I repented straight away; but the question had been asked.

"She burnt her with a poker to spoil her for showing. She was jealous." Champagne and excitement had broken down his guard so that he was not defending his mother from me any longer.

"She did it when I was out. I was going to Chichester, and then when I got the other side of Wiston I remembered something I'd forgotten and came back. I heard Dodie screaming half a mile away above the noise of the car. They were in the sitting-room when I got in, and Dodie had escaped and crawled under the book-case there, and Mother was trying to catch her. She was quite white and shaking, and the place stank of singed hair. It was horrible. I shall never forget the way poor Dodie howled."

I said nothing. For a moment the story made me feel sick.

Austin refilled our glasses, and as I looked at him his face changed. The guard was up. He had said too much and he was wondering how to cover it. When he spoke again there was a hint of argument in his soft voice.

"She said she did it because she loved me. She thought the shows upset me. You see, when I came back from France I'd been buried in a shell-hole for two days and I was half crazy. I was in hospital for months, and they gave me all sorts of treatment, electricity and massage, and suggestion. But I couldn't seem to get well, and when I came home Mother absolutely devoted herself to me. She was wonderful to me . . . wonderful. When I had my attacks she was the only person who could stop me crying. She was the only person that understood me."

His voice tailed off, and in the silence the wall-clock ticked rhythmically. He ate grapes and spat the pips with great care on to his fork. He probably still believed that he would have appendicitis if he swallowed one.

Mrs Jilks' dinner of soup, fried steak, and steam pudding, topped off with the sweet champagne, was making me feel sleepy. It had been a very long day. I thought affectionately of my bed. Austin refilled our glasses and drank again.

Probably his disability had given him a weak head for drink, and he had been over-excited by the events of the day and the conversation about Dodie. "I really never had a chance," he said suddenly. Looking at his face, damp and mottled, and at his disorganised neck-wear, it was borne in upon me that he was a little drunk.

"I never had a chance," he repeated bitterly. "It's true." And then he was off. In a low toneless voice, and for what seemed interminable hours, he talked of himself and the failure that he was, explaining, excusing, accusing, stretching himself before me on the rack of self-knowledge where he had tortured himself such countless times before.

I had not believed Austin to be a happy man. At best his existence was too circumscribed to yield him more than a dead contentment; at worst it had been bondage and frustration while his mother lived, and the broken chains still hung upon him now. What I had not realised before was that he balanced continually on the brink of despair, and that sometimes he toppled over the edge. What I did not realise until later was that when he chose he could climb out of the pit unaided; while he opened his soul to me that night I probably suffered vicariously a good deal more acutely than he did. I have found out since that Austin, despite his almost childish simplicity, was an artist in his way, making up for his physical sloth by wringing every sensation to its last dregs. He could, as it were, sit outside his own sufferings and prod himself and watch the result; he could even use his woes for his own devious ends; and his anguish was a catharsis from which he rose refreshed to play with his dogs and gluttonise on rich plum cake.

He was sorrowing just now for his lost youth in a fashion that was both painful and embarrassing.

"I was so weak," he said, "so weak. I never stood up to life. I was clever at school too, you know, quite clever . . . and good at games. Why, I was in the first fifteen." He bent his head and brooded on the crumpled vastness of his lower waistcoat.

"I wanted to be an architect," he said. "They used to say I'd make a good architect. Seems funny now, doesn't it? But I was different then. Very different. I was promising. You know, slim and pink and confident." He drank some more champagne and fell again to silent mourning. I ate grapes and tried to think of something to say which should strike the right note, bright yet consoling.

"Sometimes at night," said Austin, "when I can't sleep, I wonder where I went wrong, and I know it was all my fault really, but I don't know how. You get your hand dealt out for you, and you ought to be able to play it as well as the next man, even if it is a bad one. But if you're weak, you're weak, and you can't stand up to things. And then you're punished, punished for the way you were born. That's how it is, isn't it? But there, you're strong. You can't understand." He pointed a fork at me accusingly. The end of his tie, finally adrift from inside his waistcoat, began brushing the grape pips off his plate as he leaned forward. He was without shame, like a beggar disclosing his sores.

"I'm lazy and shiftless," he said, "and I've been an invalid for so long that I don't even want to be different. It's an excuse for having failed, you know, a fine excuse. I don't have to bother any more. I can just slop through life with as little trouble as possible. I don't want to work hard and be a famous man, or marry and have a family, because it's too much responsibility. I'm quite happy as I am, you know, most of the time. Only I don't admire myself. When I think about it I always wish I'd been different, wish I'd made myself different. But I was born weak."

He laughed. "Do you believe in predestination, Susan? It always seems to me rather like the old gag about which came first, the hen or the egg. The hen had to come out of an egg, and there had to be a hen to lay the egg. If you weren't born with the egg, so to speak . . . Hang it, I'm getting mixed. Still, you know what I mean. I was weak. I never stood up to things, never tried to stand on my own feet and make a life for myself. Now it's too late . . ."

I wished he would stop. It was useless and painful, and I still credited him with sufficient shame to believe that he would feel badly about it in the morning. I tried to change the subject, but he talked down my remarks about dogs, and I knew of nothing else that interested him. He talked on and on in the same low hopeless voice, and as he talked he popped grapes into his mouth and removed the pips on to his plate in a way that fascinated me. He was like some kind of machine.

"I was shell-shocked, Susan. You know that, don't you? So I really don't have to be quite like other people. It's none of it really my fault, is it? Except . . . except . . . Oh, damn it all, I know it really is my fault somehow. You pay for being weak just as much as you pay for being wicked . . . more, often. And I'm wicked as well as weak."

He ate the last grape and began arranging the pips in patterns on his plate, and I watched him. I had given up trying to start a normal conversation. I sat helplessly waiting for him to begin again. The wall-clock ticked loudly in the silence, making a small slithering noise with the passing of each minute. My head was beginning to ache horribly. I made a despairing effort.

"Let's go and listen to the news, Austin. It's nearly nine o'clock." He took no notice. I began to fold my napkin.

"She was dead when I found her," he remarked almost aggressively. "She was dead in bed."

"I know she was. It must have been a terrible shock for you. Try not to think of it now."

Suddenly Austin stood up. He banged his fist on the table. "She was better dead!" he shouted truculently.

My head was throbbing. I was tired beyond astonishment. Nothing, not even this, could shock or surprise me. All day long people seemed to have been talking to me, telling me things that were none of my business, being melodramatic, making scenes. Now in the heavy silence even the clock seemed to be talking.

"Dead in bed. Dead in bed. He said he found her dead in bed." It choked itself with a whirring noise. The hands pointed to nine. I pushed back my chair and rose from the table. I murmured something about listening to the wireless.

The movement seemed to rouse him. With his usual diffident politeness Austin rose also. "Certainly, Susan. Certainly. Of course. I'm sorry."

He held the door open for me and followed me into the sitting-room, and it was as if he shut the door on his sorrows and left them in the dining-room to be cleared away with the dishes. He poked the fire and tuned in the wireless carefully, and brought me cushions for my back and a stool for my feet.

But I did not hear a word that the announcer said. I was hearing suddenly the voice of Dr Lorton. "Death is seldom so considerate."

[VIII]

Austin arrived down to breakfast the next morning with no trace of hangover either alcoholic or emotional, and ate a large meal of kidney and bacon with relish. The principal actor yesterday in two painfully dramatic scenes, he was, metaphorically speaking, as fresh as a daisy, whereas I, the mere spectator, felt still exhausted. He certainly had quite remarkable recuperative powers.

He brought downstairs with him a very handsome crocodile dressing bag, which he said had belonged to his mother, and which he insisted on my taking. Perhaps, he said, as I travelled a good deal I might find it useful and he would so much like me to have it. He could do so little for me and I had been such an immense help to him.

He told me that Mrs Prioleau had always kept the case in her room, and that she had always taken special care of it. It had never been put in the boxroom with the trunks, and she had cleaned it regularly with saddle-soap. He understood that it had been a wedding-present. I was touched by the gift in spite of an inner reluctance to accept it. After all I had heard and seen, my late mother-in-law and her multitudinous belongings seemed alike rather sinister to me, and I had no great wish to own anything that had belonged to her. However it would have been ungracious to refuse, and I affected to be delighted.

"I don't know what the inside is like," Austin explained, "because it's locked and I can't find the key anywhere. She always kept it locked for some reason. In fact, I don't think I ever saw it open. Anyway a locksmith can fix it for you easily. I'd get it done myself and send it after you, only it's such a risk trusting it to the railways."

Certainly it was a beautiful bag, and from the outside it appeared almost like new. Austin said that it had hardly been used as his mother had seldom travelled.

Then he asked me about my train, and I told him that it went at eleven-thirty. He said he would drive me to the station.

Austin had the cool slyness of many rather abnormal people and it was not until we reached Chichester station that he produced Pluto and his cage, neatly tied up in paper and string, from the back of his car.

"I thought you might take him to Mary," he said blithely, "as you're going to London. He gets on my nerves so much and she wants him. She was our nurse when we were children, you know. You don't mind, do you?"

"Yes, I do mind, very much." I had already put up with a good deal from Austin, and to be burdened with his horrible parrot seemed to me just about the last straw.

"But I want to get rid of him," he wailed. "He imitates poor Mother and I can't bear it."

"Well," I said brutally, "why don't you take him yourself?"

"I couldn't. I haven't been to London for years. Susan, you've been so kind. Please take him for me. He'll be quite quiet wrapped up like this, really he will. Please do." His voice rose shrilly above the clatter of the station. With an appealing gesture he held the cage out to me. I was beginning to feel a fool. "No. No, really, Austin."

"But Susan, Dr Lorton said I ought to get rid of him. Please, you've been so good to me. And after all I *did* give you that bag of mother's." He advanced on me, still holding out the cage. I backed away. The whole station seemed to be looking at us and smiling. His voice was agonised. "I sent her a telegram. I told her you were coming. She will be so disappointed."

The train was coming in. In his other hand my brother-in-law clasped my own suitcase as a kind of hostage. "All right," I said ungraciously. He pushed me into a carriage and dumped Pluto on the seat beside me before I had time to change my mind.

"The address is on the label, 'Mrs Spencer, 76, Windermere Road.' Thank you so much, Susan. I knew you'd do it for me." The train began to move. He shook my hand. "Come again, Susan. Any time."

Crossly I thought this was quite the last thing that I would ever do. I did not wish to see Austin or his house or his dogs for the next fifty years at least, and when I reached Victoria

I would turn Pluto over to a District Messenger and be done with the horrid creature.

But things did not work out so simply. When I arrived at Victoria I was told that the Messengers were on strike. Was there any other way of having him sent? Would the railway deliver him for me? My elderly porter was an animal lover. Doubtfully he shook his head. Parrots were valuable and he might get stolen. They took cold easily and there was no saying how long he might be left hanging about. And then there was his water. It might get spilt if someone moved the cage carelessly. And was I sure he had enough seed? And didn't I think it looked like rain? Some of the delivery vans weren't covered. In short, if it was his parrot he knew what he would do.

Pluto seemed to me to be an extremely tough bird, but there had been so much fuss about him already that I could not face the possibility, however remote, of an accident befalling him while he was under my care. So the porter looked after him while I had lunch and then I took a taxi to Mrs Spencer's house.

She lived in one of a row of little red villas with a bow window and a yellowish concrete lintel over the door. Her window was full of dingy lace and geraniums, and before she ushered me into the parlour I knew just how it would smell.

She was waiting for me. She opened the door before I had time to ring the bell, and she snatched the cage out of my hand and tore off the wrappings like a child with a present.

"And here's Pluto, the darling! Pluto after all these years! Do you remember Mary now? Parrots have long memories. Come in, Mrs Prioleau. Come in Ma'm. Look at his eye now! I could pick him out of a whole zoo full, and that's a fact." Pluto regarded his new owner stonily and then squawked.

"Just listen to that now!" exclaimed Mrs Spencer in an ecstasy. "It'll be like the old days to have him waking me in the mornings. He's not a day older. And here am I that he knew when I was a girl younger than yourself! You'd hardly believe it, would you?"

She asked me to come in and have some tea. She had it ready and waiting, she said, and she was looking forward to hearing all about Mr Austin and Miss Norrie and the poor Mistress. I did not find the terms of the invitation alluring, but she seemed so disappointed when I refused that eventually, for the third time that day, I found myself doing what I had not intended. Reluctantly I paid off my taxi and abandoned myself to Mrs Spencer.

We had tea behind the lace curtains in the frowsy little parlour, full of shiny yellow cushions and holy pictures and the duplicates of the photographs Austin had shown me at Greenbarns. And Mrs Spencer talked.

Her husband had been a policeman, she told me, Irish like herself, and she was a widow and lived alone and it wasn't so often that she had company and it must be thirty years if it was a day since she'd seen a sight of any of the Family. Her husband, God rest his soul, had brought her over here to live and it was a long way away and then there were the children coming and all.

She pushed her steel-rimmed spectacles on to her forehead to get rid of the steam from her tea-cup. "It was the Mercy of Heaven," she said, "that I saw about poor Miss Helena in the paper the brussels was wrapped in, for I don't know, no more than the cat, what's been happening to them all this long time. You're Mr Austin's wife, I suppose, Ma'm?" I shuddered inwardly. "No. Henry's." Her face fell.

"I never knew Mr Henry. I left before he was born, and I never saw him above twice. I was sorry to go, and poor Miss Helena so ill when he was born too, but my John would have it. 'Take it or leave it, Mary,' he said. And what are they all doing now? . . . the children I mean, though I suppose I should hardly be calling them that."

"Well," I said doubtfully, "I'm afraid I can't tell you very much because . . ." Mrs Spencer's long upper lip curled with scorn. Silence fell between us and she stirred her tea. I had said the wrong thing. "Austin has grown very fat," I offered timidly.

"He has? Now I wonder where he'd get that from. His Da was as thin as a rail, and so was the Mistress. And he such a fine young man before he went to the war . . ."

"And Mrs Campion, Norrie, has a hat shop."

"A hat shop? And what would she be doing with a hat shop and she a lady?" Mrs Spencer sounded personally insulted. I had said the wrong thing again.

"Well, I think she needed the money. Besides, she probably wanted something to do. Lots of people keep shops these days, you know."

"Canadian trash!" My hostess sniffed. "I knew there'd be trouble there as soon as ever I heard of it. The Mistress used to write to me for a long while every Christmas, and that was how I heard. They all went off and left her in the end, all except Mr Austin. But she'd rather have had his little finger than the rest of them put together.

"I shouldn't be saying it, I suppose, but sometimes I used to feel quite sorry for poor Miss Mellie. Her Mother used to say she'd never wanted her. And she was a pretty baby too. And poor Miss Norrie! She was such a tender-hearted little mite, and after Mr Austin began to grow up Miss Helena quite changed to her. I've sometimes wondered if maybe that was why she ran off with that foreigner."

Mrs Spencer sighed. "Poor Miss Norrie! And now she sells hats! She was a dear sweet girl when I used to know her." From her tone it was evident that in her estimation no Prioleau could sink lower than keeping a shop. She asked about Melissa.

Here I told the half truth and her feelings were spared. I said that she was married and had a son and daughter and that she was an artist. No. I hadn't seen her husband or the children, but I hoped to later. "She's very well known as an artist," I said. I did not mention the divorce nor interior decorating. It would have seemed to my hostess too like house painting.

"Ah! She takes after Miss Helena then. A lovely painter she was when she was a girl, oils and watercolours and modelling in clay. But she gave it all up after she was married. She gave up most things before I left, singing and playing the fiddle and all. The Doctor, God rest his soul, he never made a joke in his life, and it was bad for her. She should never have left Ireland. Come to that, I would never have left Ireland myself with anyone but her, though John was a good husband and I've never regretted it. Will you take some more tea now, Ma'm?"

"A nice cup of tea!" interjected Pluto, breaking an offended silence for the first time.

"Her voice! Her voice to the life!" Mrs. Spencer exclaimed, and the tears came into her faded blue eyes. "Ah Pluto! You haven't changed, and that's a fact!"

To me it seemed macabre that a bird should speak with the voice of the dead, but to her simple soul it was reason only for wonder and rejoicing. She plied me with tinned salmon sandwiches which are not my favourite food at four in the afternoon, and I told her about Henry, and how I had met him when he was on leave in Christchurch and I was with friends, and how we were married by special licence when we had only known each other a fortnight, and how I had come to England afterwards when his ship was ordered home.

She was interested in him because of his mother, and because his career reflected credit on the Family, but he was born after she married and had never been her child as the others had been. Her old woman's memory slipped back into the more distant past.

"Pretty she was, and gay. She was like a light in the house with her laughing and singing, and all the lovely clothes she brought with her from Paris. But the Doctor . . . He was a good man, but not for her. He put her out the way you'd put out a candle, and never knew he was doing it.

"She could have had the pick of Dublin to choose from before the Master, her father, I mean, Mr Crawfurd, took a notion and gave away the distillery so they had nothing at all, and she wouldn't go for a companion like Miss Catherine because of her pride. Miss Catherine took after her mother, you know, but the Crawfurds, they were all wild. . . . Not wickedly wild with drink and such, but they got queer ideas into their heads sometimes and there was no shifting them. I think that was how it was with Miss Helena when she took and married the Doctor, all in five minutes and everyone on their bended knees to stop her."

There was a pause. I gathered my gloves and stood up. Mrs Spencer ignored the gesture. "Did you know she was engaged before?"

"Who? Mrs Prioleau?"

"So she was. And one of the handsomest gentlemen you'd wish to see. A lovely pair they made when they went riding together. And then . . . Well, some said he jilted her, and some said she wouldn't have him when she was poor, because she was too proud. Anyway, he went off to Africa or somewhere to fight . . . he was a captain in the army . . . and then he came back . . ."

"I'll write her such a letter!" said Pluto suddenly from the window. "Such a letter!"

Mrs Spencer's wizened face sagged with astonished horror. "For goodness sake, where did he learn that? And she that never said a cross word!"

"Perhaps someone else taught him."

"They did not. That was her voice. And what other lady would he be learning a thing like that from?"

Unfortunately Pluto was fairly launched. He eyed us wickedly as though he enjoyed the sensation he was making. "Austin!" he shouted. "Take those smelly little beasts out of my drawing-room."

"He keeps pugs," I explained lamely.

It sounds comic, but it was not. Mrs Spencer looked suddenly like a very old child whose toy has been broken. "I can't understand it," she murmured piteously. "I can't understand it at all."

There was nothing I could say. Her legend was shattered. I thanked her for my tea and pressed her hand, and trudged away with my luggage in search of a bus stop.

CHAPTER III

[I]

IT WAS QUITE by chance that I spent part of my first summer in England with Melissa and her family.

It was the summer of 1939, when the smell of war was already strong in our nostrils and we were all trying vainly to pretend that there was nothing to smell. Henry was at Portsmouth, and we had arranged to share a house a few miles out with a fellow-officer and his wife, who were prevented from joining us at the last moment.

I was very much alone at Birdhole. Henry had given up talking about what we might do on his next leave. The Navy hummed with rumours and the docks were working overtime, and his ship was being fitted as a rush job with something very new and secret. Henry himself was busy on drills and courses on gas, and we saw very little of each other except for snatched unsatisfactory evenings in Portsmouth or week-ends that seemed to pass in a flash.

It was a new sensation for me to feel lonely and without resources, but I had left my friends and my background on the other side of the world, and during my months in England I had been too much in love to make any life apart from Henry. Half-heartedly I tried to get back into journalism or begin another novel, but to English editors I was nobody, and my life had been so changed in the last year that I was not tranquil enough to settle to fiction.

Birdhole was a holiday place, too, not a place for working or for building a solitary life on gardening and the radio and good works in the village as so many English women do. There was in fact no village . . . only a scattering of summer cottages and a big white hotel where you could dance, and at the end of the season the awnings would come down and the shutters would go up, and the hotel and the bungalows would be left empty among the sandhills.

When we were there the place was full of young people, and I had plenty of acquaintances. But the married people were engrossed in their families and the unmarried ones paired off in flirtations and I seemed to belong to neither camp. Besides I could never make an engagement without the fear that Henry would come back unexpectedly or ring me up, and that I should miss him.

At the end of June Melissa wrote to Henry. She had planned to take the children to Brittany because it was cheap, but now she was afraid of being caught, and it seemed impossible to get rooms anywhere, and could Susan possibly find some place in Birdhole for them to stay. In the end with slight misgivings we invited them to share our house. "Good old Mellie," was Henry's comment. "Trust her to write if she wants something! She wants to come to us, of course. Cheap holiday—Well, she's had a pretty sticky time. . . ."

She and Barbara and Peter arrived on a hot July evening in the same bright little car that she had driven to Wiston for the funeral. It was piled high with luggage, and the occupants, having driven straight from London, looked tired and rather dirty. Melissa climbed stiffly from the driving seat, and from the seat beside her leapt the two children, chattering and jumping with excitement. They had seen the blue line of the sea and they set off towards it with the irresponsible single-mindedness of puppies.

They seemed very small to be out alone in a strange place. I asked if they would find their way back.

"They always go to the nursery school by themselves. Children ought to be independent." Melissa spoke briskly, as if she were repeating a proverb or a maxim from a copybook, but I saw the look on her face as she watched them out of sight.

We began unloading the luggage and carrying it upstairs, Melissa struggling under the weight of a large wooden box which was, she explained, Peter's collection of fossils. "He would bring it and it's very heavy. I was always so sat on as a child that I'm determined these two shall have a better time than I had, but I think butterflies would have been a pleasanter hobby."

Her cotton frock was crushed and had tea-stains on it and her make-up had gone shiny, and her fair curls straggled on the nape of her neck. She looked younger and less hard than the smart woman I remembered, but her voice still held its assertive note, as though she were on the defensive, challenging me to attack her views and way of living. I hated the thought of sharing a house with that voice for weeks. After all, Henry's family was not mine. Then suddenly, watching her nervous jerky movements, I realised that she was extremely shy, and that her manner was a facade erected against a world that frightened her. She was like Henry, without his assurance or sense of humour; she even looked like him, except that her face was older and she had the worn look of a person living under a strain. She patronised me, and yet at the same time I knew she was intensely anxious for me to like and understand her.

"I must make the children happy," she said again as we drank our tea. "We had such a horrible childhood." Too well during the weeks that followed did I come to know that refrain, repeated almost daily as an excuse for her own foibles or the misdeeds of Barbara and Peter.

Actually they were good children, and almost unnaturally sensible. But I should have liked them better without Melissa. She was passionately devoted to them both, but she dwelt on them with an almost scientific interest, noting and analysing their every movement, and yearning over each mouthful of food as though they were laboratory animals and she their keeper. There was nothing spontaneous in her relationship with them, and she had so many principles that I was always falling over a new one. Henry said that she was growing very like their father. "Only that it's Father in reverse, so to speak. His principles made him try to reform people the whole time, and she's terrified of doing the smallest thing to influence them."

It was true. Melissa's principles led her to an almost saintly forbearance in dealing with Barbara and Peter, and a self-control at which I marvelled even before I knew the effort it cost her. Only once did I see her crack, and that was the time that Peter nearly drowned himself.

We were sitting on the beach. It was high tide and windy, with waves breaking on the sands. The children were burying a dead crab one of them had found; Melissa was scrawling designs of sea-gulls on a drawing-block, and I was reading. Suddenly I heard her gasp. Her son, with the impulsive bravery of his five years, was walking deliberately into the sea. I scrambled up, but she clutched my arm, holding me back. "Let him learn," she whispered, white-faced and rigid. We must have been some fifty yards away from the children, yet she watched without cry or movement until Peter was swept off his feet and rolled over in the inevitable wave. She waded in then, and fished him out.

"A nasty old wave," he said tearfully, examining a grazed knee. His mother dabbed it with iodine, and stripped off his wet bathing dress. Her hands were shaking. "Waves won't hurt you if you're sensible. You went out too far."

"It was the undertow," explained Barbara in her small grown-up voice. "The wave sucks at your feet and then you fall over."

"You little prig!" Melissa turned on her with sudden viciousness. "Go away and play, both of you. And if you must paddle, go over to that pool." The children bustled away, looking almost as amazed as if she had struck them. She picked up her pencil with a hand that still shook.

"I suppose you think I'm a brute, Susan?" She spoke defensively. "I'm not really, you know. But I can't bring up that child as Mother brought up Austin." I said I thought she managed very well.

"Do you really, Susan? Do you? Sometimes I wonder." She scrutinised her drawing block with half-closed eyes.

"Some time ago," she said, slowly, "when Stephen left me, I realised that you never really escape from your childhood. You just react against it. My reaction hasn't been awfully successful I'm afraid. You see, Mother made such a terrible hash of everything . . . her own life, us, being married to Father . . . that I determined I'd do quite differently. I never gave up anything because I was married. I had my business . . . I'd built it up myself, and it certainly stood to me well enough, at least until this Hitler business started to blow up . . . People don't want to decorate their houses when they may be bombed almost any time . . . and I never let anything interfere with it. Well, at least Father didn't walk out on Mother like Stephen did on me, and goodness knows he would have had every excuse." She shrugged her shoulders. "Anyway, that's all over now. He offered to come back for the sake of the children, but I wouldn't have it. We were quarrelling before he went away, and I'd had enough of quarrels in the home. The children were too young to know anything about the divorce and so it didn't affect them. It cut me up at the time, because I'd had an idea that I was being rather clever over everything, and of course I was fond of him. Now I don't care any more, except that it *is* so difficult bringing up children alone. I try to avoid the faults in our own upbringing, and then I go too far the other way."

Pensively she added another seagull to the collection on her block.

"You see, Susan, ours was such an odd family . . . at least I think it was, though sometimes I wonder if most families aren't odd when you get to know them. Only in our house there always seemed to be something wrong . . . something under the surface. It sounds melodramatic I know, but looking back it always seemed to me as though Mother had some sort of queer secret. She used to look at Father sometimes in the most peculiar way, with her eyes half shut, as if she had her foot on a man-trap and was wondering whether to spring it on him.

"She used to make terrible scenes sometimes over nothing at all, and you could feel them brewing like a storm. It made me feel insecure all the time, and any psychologist will tell you how bad that is for children. She'd pick on one of us or one of the maids, and fly into a rage about some perfectly idiotic thing until she had whoever it was provoked into answering back . . . generally if it was a maid she gave notice. Then Mother was the aggrieved person, and the odd part was that by the end you generally thought she was, and begged her pardon humbly because she had behaved quite outrageously. To this day I don't know how she did it. It must have been the charm old Galvain talks so much about. The maids adored her, and they always took back their notice in the end.

"She was an out-and-out sadist . . . verbally I mean . . . and a bit of a masochist too. Even as a child I always realised that she got some sort of queer fun out of weeping and wailing and forgiving us for what we hadn't done. She generally gave us presents too, and we were nothing if we weren't practical . . . Henry and I, that is. Norrie minded dreadfully."

I asked how their Mother had treated Austin. It seemed to me that an upbringing such as Melissa described would account for a good deal of his queerness.

"Oh, she never went for him. She adored him. Oedipus complex, of course." Melissa waved her pencil. The colour had come back into her cheeks and once more she was her dogmatic self. "She was in love with him," she said.

"What was Austin like when he was young?" I asked her idly. To imagine him as a child was an effort, rather like trying to think of a baby brontosaurus.

"He wasn't so bad then, except that he was so terribly spoilt. Do you know, he joined up when he was only sixteen? He gave a false age, and Father encouraged him, which was comic considering the fetish he made of telling the truth. He said it made him feel that he really was doing something to help beat the Germans. But Mother . . ." Dramatically Melissa outlined the upheaval that resulted from Austin's one successful effort at self-assertion. Mrs Prioleau stormed and cried and accused her family of being murderers, and wore black for months, as though her son were already dead. And Dr Prioleau gave him a special mention in family prayers as "Thy servant Austin, who is now numbered among Thy Crusaders."

"Most of the time," Austin's sister commented acidly, "he was crusading on Salisbury Plain, but that made no difference to either of them."

Melissa had however, gained some small credit at school by boasting about her hero brother. "Norrie and I were always boastful, because we felt kind of pariahs. We never had any money to spend, or anything nice to wear . . . and we could never ask anyone to the house. So we were always whistling to keep our courage up. That's why I spoil Peter and Barbara so much, I suppose. I want them to feel normal and sure of themselves, not like we were."

Austin went to France in due time, and in the 1918 retreat he was reported wounded and missing. "And then," said Melissa brutally, "Mother really enjoyed herself. She was genuinely unhappy, but she always loved a situation. She swore he was alive, and do you know, Susan, she'd hardly left the house for ten years, but she went touring round all the hospitals worrying everybody till they produced him for her. He'd lost his memory. Oh, she was fond of him all right, even if she never cared tuppence for the rest of us."

Melissa spoke with a deep bitterness. Her jealous sense of injury rankled through the years like a chronic itch that she must always be scratching. She could not let the past rest, and even now, when her mother was dead and the home she had hated was broken, she must still be harping back to it, taking it apart with a kind of fascinated loathing as though she were dissecting a disgusting insect.

Through her eyes I saw something of the sinister discomfort of the house by the river . . . the silent attics, full of rubbish and spiders, the creaking boards and the empty rooms; the stairs where the rats walked at nights, going plop, plop, plop on the treads, the scummy water lapping the end of the blackened little garden, the trains roaring on the bridge above. And Mrs Prioleau shutting from her her other children and the stern ailing husband she disliked, fixing her mind and will and energy like a burning-glass upon the wreck of her elder son.

She never left him day or night. He dared not be alone. She slept in the dressing-room off his bedroom to calm him down when he woke at nights and her days were passed in the most patient efforts to amuse him.

"She was never out of temper with him," Melissa said grudgingly. "I must say that for her. And he was simply maddening sometimes. He used to sit for hours with his head in his hands, saying he was a failure and he had better be dead, and when he talked, he talked the whole time about himself. He was self-centred in a way that no normal person could be, however selfish they were. It was his mental state we knew, but the only person who could stand him was Mother, and what was so extraordinary was that in other things she never had seemed to have any self-control at all. There were no more rows with anyone else either. I suppose she had enough to occupy her without them. Well . . ."

Melissa broke off. She was gazing at Peter who was poised, rather dangerously it seemed, on a high piece of pointed rock. He looked at us unhappily, his mouth open for the first sob. His mother shouted at him. "You got up there," she said, "and you can jolly well get down!" Anxiously he looked down to the comfortable sand below him, and then slowly and carefully began to climb from his perch.

"See what it's like, Susan?" Her voice was sad. "He's all right this time, as it happens, but he might have fallen and hurt himself badly. He's so tiny still. Only . . . I simply daren't. When I think of how Mother undermined Austin . . . with the best will in the world . . ."

She was astride her hobby-horse again, the faithful steed that she mounted whenever anything happened to upset her. As she talked she twisted her pencil maddeningly, and her eyes blinked as though she was on the verge of tears.

"I know it's quite different. Peter's a child, and he was an adult and shell-shocked as well. But it began a long time before. She coddled him from a baby. Afterwards when he was like that she ought to have helped him stand on his own feet, but she never did. Father told her repeatedly that she was doing all the wrong things, but she wouldn't listen. He never expected she would. Austin was happy, she said, and wasn't that the main thing?

"Then when he was better he wanted to train as an architect. She stopped him. She told him he would never be fit to earn his own living, that there was no need for him to bother because she and father had enough to keep him. I was only a kid, but I remember the fuss about it all. Father was too ill to stand up to her, and Austin caved in, of course. He sat back on her, and that was fine. She was quite happy and I think he was too, after a time.

"My God, Susan! I suppose I'm bitter because I'm a thwarted woman who couldn't keep her husband, but when I think of Mother I hate her for what she did to us. Look at the hash poor Norrie made too, running off with Campion. Henry's the only one of us that's really normal."

It was nearly one o'clock. Like a volcano that has finished erupting, Melissa subsided, looking even a little ashamed of her outburst.

"I shouldn't have spoken like that," she said to me later. But the next time she had trouble with Peter she was off again. I was not sorry to think that they would soon be going back to London.

"Unless war breaks out," she remarked with ghastly cheerfulness, "I shall have to stay here then. I can't go home with the children." I knew she was lying awake worrying about Barbara and Peter, because she told me so. "You don't know what it's like, Susan," she assured me in tones of mingled smugness and anxiety. "You have no children." It was natural perhaps, though irritating, that she did not feel that I had any reason for worrying over the war. She was nothing if not single-minded.

The beginning of that September remains with me like the dim memory of a nightmare. The frothy friendly gaiety of Birdhole vanished in a stream of hurrying cars. People were recalled to their jobs, to the army, the navy, the territorials. They went to join up in this or that, urged equally by patriotism, the famous English "sporting spirit," and the herd instinct that grips almost everyone in moments of crisis. One caught glimpses of them as they went, wearing unfamiliar clothes and serious expressions.

Only the mothers and young families stayed, Birdhole being considered a safe area, and the departing cars were passed on the road to London by other cars, full of children and old people and dogs and luggage being driven to sanctuary, away from the bombs that threatened London.

Melissa and her family stayed in the bungalow, and I travelled to London on the Monday, in a slow and crowded train with blue paint on the light bulbs.

Henry had disappeared and I did not know where to write to him. I had no idea when or where I should see him again, if I ever did. I tried to join the W.R.N.S., the W.A.A.F., the A.T.S. and was refused because of my heart, which I once strained swimming and which has never quite returned to normal.

In the end I found myself doing a rather dull clerking job in connection with evacuation. It was a very long time before I thought much again either of Melissa or Austin, still less of that strange woman, their mother, whose character, even in death, lay like a distorting shadow across the lives of all her children except Henry.

[II]

When I was a school girl I once over-ate on sardines, and for months afterwards I could hardly bear to look at one. Mentally my visit to Austin had much the same effect on me, and although I wished him no harm, and indeed felt sorry for him, especially after what Melissa had told me, I never wanted to set eyes on him again. My mission had been a failure. He remained at Greenbarns, and, if his mother's effects were ever cleared up it was not by me. Neither did I care. I had had enough and too much of the whole business.

But Austin had not had enough of me. Oddly enough, since my visit had apparently done nothing except annoy and upset him, he longed to see me again. He wrote three times during the summer, once inviting me to a dog-show, and twice imploring me to come down and stay with him. Wiston was beautiful in the summer, he said, and we could visit so many interesting places in the car. I wrote politely mendacious refusals and salved my conscience with a vague invitation to Birdhole, which I knew he would not accept because it meant leaving the dogs. Then war broke out and I forgot all about him.

Just before Christmas he called at my office. He was announced as Captain Prioleau, and for an instant my heart leapt, thinking that the office girl was promoting Henry. Then I looked up. Before me, self-consciously splendid in khaki, stood my brother-in-law.

"I thought you'd like to see me in my uniform," he said, and gravely, like a child in its party clothes, he displayed himself front, back and sides. The two girls who shared my office goggled in an astonishment of which he was quite unconscious. "I think it's a very nice cut," he said solemnly. "Don't you agree?"

I nodded, speechless. Considering what was inside the uniform the tailor had done very well.

But Austin himself was improved beyond belief, and that not only by his fine feathers. He was thinner and a better colour, and his sparse hair was draped carefully over the bald patch, and his collar looked clean, though that may have been because it was not originally a white one. There was a crease in his trousers and a shine on his shoes. (Capital chap, you know, my batman!) He was wholly delighted with himself.

He chose lunch for me quite simply by picking the most expensive dishes on the menu, and he was so obviously pleased with my company that my heart melted. But when he told me that he was training, I was so flabbergasted that I blurted out, "Whatever for?" The word suggested to me youths in shorts and singlets running down country lanes or doing breathing exercises at open windows. It was simply not applicable to Austin, even in uniform.

A pained expression passed over his face. “Troops, you know. Knock ’em into shape.” He stuck out his two top chins and tried to look tough.

The job seemed so wildly improbable that I forbore to ask how he got it. I could only think that his senior officer had drawn him in a lottery.

“We old ’uns,” he said, throwing out his chest, “we’ll show ’em.” Now that he had given up being an invalid he was quite aggressively healthy.

I asked him about the dogs and he told me that Mrs Jilks was looking after them for the present. He did not sound in the least bit interested in them. He talked of the call of duty and was very blood-thirsty and patriotic.

Characteristically he seemed to have forgotten that I had known him formerly in a less heroic role. But he was so transparent that once again I found myself liking him, even though it was clear that he was not in the least interested in me except as an audience. All he wanted was that I should listen while he told me about “Training,” and he told me in the same exhaustive detail as he had once told me about pug dogs, arranging bits of bread on the table-cloth and drawing diagrams to illustrate his points.

In his new character of warrior he had developed an infantile liking for practical jokes, and his monologue was sprinkled with trivial anecdotes which were also occasionally funny. Soda-water siphons figured largely, and beds in their most innocent connotation, and the moral of everything was that he was a fine fellow in a world of fine fellows, loud laughers, deep drinkers, men of action.

But he was not entirely a changed man. Traces of the old bondage were upon him for all his new-found assurance, and he spoke hectoringly to the waiter as people do who are not quite sure of themselves. And then, at the end of a particularly arch little story about what he had said to the colonel, "Poor Mother!" he remarked suddenly. "She would have a fit if she could see me now."

I said that I thought she would be very pleased, but he shook his head lugubriously. "Not she."

"But you're so well. You're looking so well."

"Yes. But she wouldn't believe it. She'd be thinking of my heart or my chest or my nerves. And the odd part is that when I lived with her I was never well. Too little exercise." He pondered, munching grapes in the familiar way and arranging the pips on his plate.

"She was wonderful," he said, "wonderful. I should never be here if it hadn't been for her." His voice was low, with the slight impediment that I remembered. He spoke like a person repeating a lesson. For a moment I had the odd impression that I was watching a Jekyll and Hyde performance, a species of shape-shifting by which Austin slipped back into his old flabby self. Then his expression changed. "They're such good chaps," he said inconsequentially. We had returned to "Training".

"Austin," Norrie said later, when I told her of the meeting, "Austin is a 'Joiner' by nature. He's a Rotarian, an Ancient Buffalo, an Old Boy. He has the herd instinct very strongly. And Mother never let him have it. That's why he stuck to those dreadful little dogs in the old days, because the shows gave him some excuse for getting away and being boys together, even if he could only be boys with retired gents and leather-faced women in dirty mackintoshes."

There was probably a lot in what she said. Several people in their different ways and their own peculiar idioms had summed up for me Austin's relationship with his mother, and always to the same effect. Even the mad Miss Trip had seen him as her prey, her willing and unconscious victim.

"I expect," I said to Norrie, "that Dr Lorton shifted him in the end."

"I expect he did," she said. But we never discovered for certain.

Austin always made out that he had been moved only by patriotism. But he let slip the information that Dr Lorton was a member of the local Army Medical Board, and later on he mentioned that Greenbarns had been taken by the military on the outbreak of war.

"So really," Norrie concluded, "he had to do something about it." We smiled together over Austin and his newest toy. It was quite impossible somehow to regard him as a hero.

[III]

"When I ran away to sea," remarked Henry, pulling viciously at a thigh boot, "when I ran away to sea, I never thought of anything like these ruddy convoys. Out and home—out and home, like a bloody commercial, and I wanted romance and the tropics." His voice was muffled as he pulled the final jersey over his head. Emerging, he remarked with tardy tactfulness that of course he hadn't thought of getting married in those days.

It was a bitterly cold winter morning with no hint of dawn behind the blackout, and as he dressed I shivered round our bedroom collecting the last of his belongings. "Pipe. Matches. Got your flashlight, dear? Drink up your tea. You're forgetting it."

Time had not reconciled me to the dreary litany of those few moments before he left me . . . left me perhaps for the last time. We never spoke of it, and I sometimes wondered how he felt himself. Probably his mind was entirely occupied in getting himself to the docks, for nature had not intended him for an early riser.

He drank his tea in three gulps and looked at the alarm clock. "Good heavens, Susie! Is that the time?" Came the final scuffle and the note of anguish in his voice. "Where are my gloves? No, not those! I'll miss that flaming bus. And my muffler? Thanks. 'Bye, darling. I'll be seeing you soon. Don't you worry."

He was gone in a rush of heavy boots and swinging gas-mask, and the door was shut behind him, shut on my life for a fortnight, a month. . . . Already he would be running down the dark street, bundled with his equipment, dodging the first labourers on their way to work. Now he would be in the bus, fumbling in his pocket for change, lighting his first cigarette, drawing on it till the gloom showed his face in a relief map of heights and black hollows. Now he was going through the docks, splashing through the fishy puddles with their film of oil, passing the barbed wire and the sentry with the flash-lamp. Now he was going on board. . . Now . . .

But from there onwards I was ignorant, and imagination, starved of nourishment, refused to serve me longer. Being a literal-minded person, Henry included me in all the warnings about careless talk, and I knew nothing whatever about his life at sea. The door which shut behind him shut him from me almost as though he were dead. I could not write to him or hear from him, or even picture to myself what he might be doing at a given hour or in what hostile waters.

Yet I was not unhappy while he was away from me. I had been through so much already that I expected very little, and I knew that I was lucky just to have him alive and to be able to see him sometimes. In the first year of the war we had hardly seen each other at all, and after that his ship had struck a mine and he had been missing for nearly a month, making a compulsory journey to Newfoundland on a rescuing tramp, outward bound and with no wireless. His arm had been broken in the explosion and had to be reset when he got back to England, and he was on sick-leave with it for seven weeks, and I was happier with him then than I had ever been before in my whole life. I had mourned him for dead, and he had come back again when I had given up hoping. Since then I felt, for no reason at all, that whatever happened I should never lose him again.

I was not lonely. I worked in the W.V.S. Canteen by the docks, and packed parcels for prisoners of war, and met other service wives for bridge and cups of coffee and parties to the cinema. I was never quite alive when he was away, but I put on a fairly good act.

Seven o'clock in the morning. The inn was astir, and below my window the symphony of the day's traffic was beginning with the roar of lorries and the shuddering of buses as they stopped and started. Snuggled back in the still warm bed I lay in the darkness and wondered with incurious drowsiness why Henry had never told me that he had run away to sea. He had told me about Dartmouth and his first ship, and about a girl in Malta whom he had nearly married before he met me, but I knew nothing whatever about this particular escapade. I had always understood that his entry into the Navy as well as his subsequent career had been completely orthodox. Strange to be married to a man, and to love him, and yet to know so little of him!

Once again I thought of that cold spring morning, nearly two years ago, when I had stood by the open coffin where Henry's mother lay and wondered what spirit had lighted the old impassive face with its elusive likeness. It must have hurt her when Norrie ran away to be married! And Henry, too, running off to sea. And Melissa who hated her, so that her voice was unsteady when she spoke of home. And Austin! I wondered how much Mrs Prioleau had understood, whether she knew how deeply she had failed with her children.

Henry came back on the eleventh day, tired and happy and shouting for a bath. No. Nothing had happened. All very dull except that they'd been nearly rammed in a fog, and Sparks had started measles. At his age, poor chap. A rotten show! Definitely! Covered in spots, too! They'd bunged him off to an isolation hospital somewhere.

That night I asked Henry about running away to sea, and he threw back his head and laughed. "Good Lord, Susie! Didn't I ever tell you that? It was a poor show, and no mistake!"

It seems that when Dr Prioleau died Henry's mother thought she would make him into a doctor. "I think in some funny sort of way she felt she owed it to him, though why she should have Lord only knows, for I wasn't good at books, and I'd never cared for Father enough to want to be like him, and I'd have made a pretty poor doctor one way and another.

"Well, she was always talking about it as if it was fixed and settled, and I used to get quite worried. I was just about thirteen then, and reading the *Boys' Own Paper* like mad, and you know what an ass you are at that age. Well, one day I just hooked it."

Henry's inspiration had been a serial story in which the hero, a member of the landed gentry, repaired the family fortunes after his father's death, by shipping as a cabin boy on a schooner bound for the South Seas. He met many hardships, of course, but he endured them all with Christian fortitude, returning on the last page, bronzed and stalwart, to his widowed mother, carrying the pirates' hoard of doubloons and pieces of eight in an iron-bound chest on his shoulder.

Everything, except possibly the widowed mother, had appealed mightily to Henry, especially since their house was near the river and his favourite occupation for years had been hanging over the railings of Hungerford Bridge to watch the shipping. So one morning he took his money-box and the contents of his Mother's handbag and slipped away to the Pool of London.

No one there thought much of him as a prospective cabin-boy, and his efforts at playing the old salt met with obvious failure, easily enough explained by the discovery that he was still wearing his school cap. He threw it away, but even that didn't help much, so then he decided that his costume was all wrong.

The owner of the first slop shop told him to "run home to Mum now, there's a good boy!", but at the second shop he tried he bought a pair of long blue trousers and some second-hand seaboots and a white muffler.

"And then," said Henry, "I had another bright idea. Someone had called me a toff, and I thought it must be my accent that was wrong, so I went into a corner and started trying to talk common. But it didn't work very well, because I felt such a fool, and I knew I should forget to drop my aitches if I got excited. I was pretty browned off by then, and I didn't dare go home because of the money and throwing my cap away. Besides, I was as pleased as Punch over the docks . . . I'd never been there before . . . and I wanted to go to sea more than ever."

So he went into an eating-house, and had dinner and half a pint of beer, which made him feel very manly, and listened to the talk between the proprietor and the other customers. They were nearly all sailors of some sort, and they came from every part of the country, and he sat and practised their accents under his breath until someone noticed him and pointed him out to a friend, and they began laughing. Whereupon Henry, becoming extremely embarrassed, paid his bill and rushed out of the place. At the door he bumped into two sailors and heard one say to the other, "I think we go in here to eat. Yes?"

This was his solution. The *Boys' Own Paper* was full of people, generally villains, who talked broken English, and it was much easier than talking cockney or Yorkshire. Besides, if anyone asked you awkward questions you could pretend not to understand. Emboldened by the beer, he asked the next passer-by "Vair ees de Souree Doaks?" and the man did not appear to be in the least amused or even surprised. He raised his voice and spoke slowly to Henry, explaining that he should ask a policeman, and what a policeman looked like, and Henry was enchanted with himself. He was tall for his age, he said, and probably looked quite a passable young sailor in the new trousers. An earnest reader of John Buchan, he bit his finger nails, never a strong point with him anyway, and rubbed dirt into them to make his hands look work-worn, and started anew on his quest.

Naturally, very few of the men whom he asked were in a position to hire cabin-boys, and fewer still wanted one on the spot. The only two who did asked him difficult questions about papers, of which he knew nothing, and turned with a shrug from his protestations of "me no spik de English ver goot."

He was wondering disconsolately how you became a stowaway when an elderly man asked him how he would like to go fishing. Henry jumped at the offer. The boat, as it happened, was not going fishing. She was a small tramp bound for Lerwick with a mixed cargo, and the boy had just been taken to hospital with a crushed hand. The master wanted someone in a hurry, and Henry could come to Shetland if he liked, and no bother at all. He went.

Poor Henry! His first experience as a sailor was not very successful. He felt extremely sick before the "Jolly Lass" was fairly into the North Sea, and much of his time was spent in frying fat pork or steak and onions on a smoky oil stove in a horribly dirty little cabin, which did nothing to improve his condition. To add to his troubles, on the second day out he tripped over a coil of rope while he was carrying a bucket of dirty water, and not only spilt the water all over himself, but blacked his eye severely on the bucket handle. Everyone was kind, he said, but they seemed to find it all much funnier than he did.

He never got to Shetland. His mother missed first her money and then her son, and after twenty-four hours she told the police . . . "for the look of the thing, I expect," he said, with a cynicism largely unconscious. Little boys who run away from home are generally sought, among other places, at the nearest port, and Henry's movements had been rather conspicuous. When the "Jolly Lass" put into Hull the police collected him and he was returned ignominiously to his mother.

"And how did you feel?"

"Flat," said Henry. "It took us four days to get to Hull, and I'd been sick most of the time, and my eye was all bunged up, and I'd caught a perfectly terrible cold. I didn't want to go home, but I wasn't exactly sorry to have to leave the 'Jolly Lass.' Though of course I wouldn't have gone if the bobby hadn't made me."

A policeman with a tendency to moralise delivered him to Mrs Prioleau, and if she had been nicer to him he would have gone back meekly to school and settled down when the time came to being a doctor or anything else that was suggested to him. He felt for the moment quite certain that he was not cut out for a nautical career.

I asked if his mother had scolded him.

"Oh, no. She wasn't in a scolding mood. She simply didn't seem to mind whether I came back or not. She was reading a book when I was brought in and she only said I'd better have a bath. She wasn't even cold," said Henry, "just not awfully interested. She never said a word about the money, either. I'd far rather she'd been angry."

Two days later Henry's godfather turned up. Dr Prioleau was only recently dead, and it was probably a business visit. He was much interested in Henry's black eye, and made detailed enquiries as to its origin. He chuckled over the story, doubtless told only in its baldest outlines, and then asked point-blank if Henry still wanted to be a sailor. Defiantly, because he felt nobody loved him and he hated being laughed at, Henry answered that he did, and the next thing he knew was that his godfather, who was a Very Important Person of some sort, had arranged for him to have special tuition and for his name to go forward for the next entrance examination for Dartmouth College.

I asked what his mother had said to this, and he shrugged his shoulders. "Oh, she was far too wrapped up in Austin to care what happened to me," he said. "My godfather more or less adopted me after that, and I was hardly ever home again. Suited me all right."

I recalled Melissa's remark that Henry was the only normal one of the family because he had escaped early enough. Except in a negative way, the late Mrs Prioleau had certainly left singularly little impression on her younger son.

[IV]

In August 1941 Henry transferred to submarines. He was delighted, but I was not. Convoy work in those days was dangerous enough, but at least if the worst happened you generally knew it within a reasonable time. Now, if he went, I should never know more than the bleak little message heard so often over the radio: "The submarine Blank is overdue at her base and must be presumed lost. The next of kin have been informed." Less than ever now, if he died, would I know how or when or if he had suffered much. The fine confidence that had sustained me hitherto failed me badly in the first few weeks after he had gone.

The strolling policeman, the telegraph boy on his rounds, the letter in an unknown writing, the telephone ringing late at night or early in the morning, could all be harbingers of disaster. Even the half-remembered uncomfortable dream took on a new significance. Henry had died to me a hundred times before he was well out of home waters.

There was no reason for me to remain any longer in our lodgings since his port of call had been changed, and so I went to London. Within three days I had found a post with the Ministry of Information.

It was a good post, on the Dominions side. Luck, my training as a journalist, and a chance meeting with an old friend of my father's who happened to know someone in high places, produced it for me quite unexpectedly, and I found it so interesting that most of the time I did not worry about Henry any more, or at least not consciously.

My job was to "sell" New Zealand to the British public, to tell them in lectures and articles how we lived over there and what our country was like and what it was doing to help the war. I had an office and a secretary and a private telephone line. I attended meetings and receptions, and felt almost ashamed of myself sometimes because I enjoyed it all so much. The only trouble was that as the work grew I found myself more and more tied to my desk, while the work I liked best, travelling round speaking, was done by other people.

During these months in London I came to know Henry's elder sister Norrie. When I first came up I sought her advice on the subject of flats and she was very helpful; later on when a bomb broke all my windows and smashed the water main, she invited me to stay with her out at Hampstead. She said that she did it because she so liked company when she had to sit in a public shelter, but this was nonsense since she very seldom left her house during a raid. She grew to like my company, raid or no raid, I think, but at the beginning she had me to live with her out of pure kindliness and in memory of the days when she herself had been lonely among the crowds of New York.

She rarely spoke of herself. Indeed she was not a great talker, and when we were together we were generally too busy or too tired to indulge in much conversation. I think that in a way she rather despised herself for making hats while other people were making bombs, but, as she said, hats helped to keep people cheerful, so that it really was war-work of a sort, and anyway she was being as patriotic as she could afford to be without a private income. If she gave up "Leonore" where would she be when the war ended? Anyway, she was too old a dog to learn new tricks.

I felt a little curious sometimes about her early life, remembering the fragments that Henry and Melissa had told me and the dark sayings of Mrs Spencer, but it was too delicate a subject for idle probing, and I had lived with Norrie for nearly two months before she told me anything whatsoever about it. When she did she told me a lot.

We had both of us had a bad day. Her forewoman had given notice, and one of her best assistants had just received calling-up papers. I had had a difference of opinion with my chief, and had lost a new glove on the way home. It was weeks since I had had word of Henry and I was beginning to sleep badly. In the sitting-room of the flat, when we came back in the evening, we were greeted by a note from the daily woman, telling us that she was evacuating her children to the country and could not come again. We cooked and ate our supper in morose and weary silence.

"Well," said Norrie, looking at the array of dirty plates, "I was a professional dishwasher once, so I suppose I can cope with this."

"Were you?"

"My God, I was." I waited for further revelations, but none came. We washed up together. She was as quick as lightning.

Then the barrage opened. It was a raid on South London, not near enough to drive us to shelter but far too loud for it to be worth while trying to sleep when the time came. We sat by the dying fire drinking tea and smoking, and suddenly Norrie reverted to the subject of dish-washing. Partly, I suspect, because she wanted to take my mind off my own troubles, partly perhaps from the desire that comes even to reserved people to talk of themselves, she began to speak of those old days in New York.

"It was after I ran away from Philip," she said, "in 1921, and it kept me from starving. It didn't last long, but it was long enough. Plates, and plates, and plates, and the whole place sopping with water and smelling of grease and steam, and six of us washing like mad. And the clatter and heat of it! When we'd done the dishes we used to start on the saucepans. Sometimes I didn't get home till midnight. But I got out of it all right." I asked her how.

"A pick-up. A man in the street who noticed my figure . . . it was rather good in those days . . . and offered me a job modelling gowns. He wanted me for more than a model, of course, but it was better than dishes. We were very fond of each other, really, only he had a wife and a kind of New England conscience. He gave me a start, though, set me up in my first shop as soon as I had enough experience. I'd always liked hats, you see, because I'm interested in faces."

I said I had always believed the streets of New York were paved with gold in those days, and that no one needed to wash dishes or starve. Norrie laughed.

"My good Susan! You've no idea what I was like in those days! Besides I came there with no clothes barring the ones I was wearing, which weren't up to much, and then I had my handbag snatched. I had to take the first job that came my way, and it happened to be dish-washing. *Voilà tout!*" She waved her plump hands expressively.

The distant barrage suddenly died down. In the silence we heard a car drive through the empty street, probably an ambulance.

"We ought to go to bed," Norrie said, and lighted another cigarette. The noise began again, shaking the windows and door. I poured myself some more tea.

"Of course"—her voice was thoughtful—"only someone very green would ever have fallen for Philip Etienne. I was as green as the grass in spring-time. Funny!" And she told me about it.

She was seventeen when war broke out in 1914, and she had never been further afield than a visit to Oxford or to her grandparents in Ireland. She had taken her first-aid examination at school, and as soon as she left, at Christmas, her father announced that she would work as a V.A.D. He did not offer her an alternative, because that was not his way. She went to Millbank.

She lived at home and walked to her work, daily or nightly. In her spare time, such as it was, she worked as her father's dispenser. It hardly occurred to her for some time that her life was circumscribed, because she had never known it otherwise, and was too busy to think about it very much, anyway.

"You see, Susan, it was never really suggested in our house that anyone ought to enjoy themselves. Mother never went anywhere or took us anywhere, and Father was always busy. We never could ask any of our friends home when we were at school because Mother said it gave her headaches, and no one ever thought of buying us anything because it was pretty. When bobbed hair came in Mellie and I cut off each other's pigtails as a protest against having them tied with tape. We didn't do it very well, but Father said it was probably quite hygienic, and Mother didn't appear to notice."

So Norrie passed the four years of the war in preparing trays and making beds and emptying slops, and then at the end of 1918, when the flow of wounded slackened, she began to look round.

"I think I just developed slowly," she explained. "Quite honestly I wasn't interested in men. I had horrid clothes and I didn't know how to put them on, and I thought the V.A.D.s who went out with officers were rather fast. I heard a good many doubtful jokes, naturally, and some fairly lurid gossip, but it all went in at one ear and out of the other. I must have been a god-awful prig."

And then she met Philip Etienne Campion. He had not been wounded on the field of battle, but he had been rolled on very thoroughly by a mule, which was nearly as good. He was encased in plaster almost from head to foot, and she used to help him with his meals. He was very handsome, and very nearly as lonely as she was. The wards were beginning to empty, and the nurses had more time to be interested in individual patients. Norrie became exceedingly interested in Captain Campion.

"It was his foreign accent that did it, of course. If he'd merely spoken English like a Canadian I'd have lumped him with the others and just called him a 'colonial,' and I should have known that he shouldn't have hated shaving quite so much, and that he was a hick in spite of his pips and his grand stories. But he was a Canuck, and he spoke the most romantic broken English, and so when he began to take me out it seemed all right when he didn't know which fork to use and went through doors in front of me."

Norrie said that she had never made up her mind whether Philip was simple or just a liar. He may have been a bit of both. Perhaps homesickness had made him believe in the paradise he told her of; perhaps he deliberately invented it out of vanity and because he was so anxious for her to marry him. One thing that she was sure of was that he had no more idea than she of the gulf between her standards and his. His whole life had been spent first on his father's farm and then in army camps and in the trenches. He had, as she said, never seen a plug that pulled until he came to the hospital.

His bride worked in the hospital ward, doing often rough and unpleasant work. She wore uniform, and when she went out with him her clothes were plain and dowdy. In the garish splendour of a Corner House she was as overawed as he was. Unintentionally she probably cheated him as much as he cheated her. Things might have been very different if she could have invited him to her home.

They were married secretly on the morning of the day he sailed for Canada. Norrie had put off telling her parents about Captain Campion, because she dreaded the scene her mother might make. Years of these scenes with their tears and recriminations and hysterical forgivenesses had broken her nerve so that she would tell any number of lies rather than risk a truth which might displease. When she had gone out with him she had always invented a story about a girl friend, and by the time the question of marriage came up, she was far too deeply involved in lies and far too scared to act otherwise than as she did.

He was going on a troopship, but he left her money for her passage and she followed him, stealing from her parents' house early one morning with a note left behind to tell them what she had done. Until the morning that she ran away they never so much as knew the existence of Captain Philip Etienne Campion.

"I'd asked for it," said Norrie, "and I got it. Philip hadn't even a house of his own. We just lived with his parents. They were peasant farmers and they lived like peasant farmers, and they took it for granted that I should live the same way. Their ancestors may have been noblemen of France, but they'd travelled a bit since then.

"I'll never forget that place, not if I live to be a hundred. I'll never forget the night I arrived, and the smell of the kitchen when we came in. It wasn't really dirty, but they had the fly screens up and there was onion soup on the fire, and Philip's father was smoking a strong pipe, and I'd been sick in the train. *And* I had been thinking of the lovely bath I would have when I got to the ancestral hall.

"Bath! There wasn't even a well. The water was hauled up from the lake in barrels, and in the winter we cut blocks of ice and hauled them up instead. Bath, indeed!" She chuckled.

"And the odd part of it was that Philip Etienne just couldn't realise I'd expected anything different. We slept in the loft of the shed where they kept the cow and the horse, and some odd chickens too, in the winter, and he pointed out to me that their breath would help warm the place when it was cold." Her nose wrinkled disgustedly. "They said they never cleaned the byres till the ice went out on the lake, because the animals were warmer that way."

I made some fatuous remark about love in a cottage. Norrie considered. "You mean, 'When poverty comes in at the door love flies out of the window'? No. It wasn't like that. I'd just been in love with someone that didn't exist. Philip was a peasant who had been polished up a little by his commission and the polish hadn't lasted. We had nothing in common, not even language.

"They use to talk patois, and I didn't understand one word in five, and they couldn't understand my French, such as it was, either. If he spoke in English his parents got suspicious and thought we were making fun of them. And I couldn't milk. That was a terrible blow. We all did our best, I think, but it was hopeless from the start. There was the priest, too. We'd been married in a registry office, and he raised hell because I was a heretic and we were living in sin. And I turned obstinate."

Philip Etienne left the farm in the autumn. He went north to work in a lumber camp until the thaw came; the money that he earned there would pay for the few luxuries in the poor farm-house, for new pots and pans and shirts and boots. Norrie, six months pregnant, sick and unhappy, cried and implored him to stay, not so much because she loved him, but rather that she could hardly bear the thought of spending the winter alone with his parents.

The baby was born in January, and she was very ill. "I hoped I'd die, but I didn't. We couldn't get a midwife because of the snow, and Philip's mother went in for all sorts of magic nonsense when she should have been coaxing it alive. So that was that. But they seemed to think it was my fault that it never breathed.

"I tried to kill myself afterwards by going into the snow, but I fell into a drift and the old man found me and brought me back. They thought it was fever and gave me a lot of revolting things to drink."

In her first months of loneliness Norrie had written home, lying letters telling how happy she was. Her father answered coldly, for he was deeply hurt. Her mother sent her one letter of violent abuse, followed by an occasional perfunctory note. Only Aunt Catherine read between the glowing lines of Norrie's writing. She sent her niece an extremely fierce letter, and enclosed fifty dollars in it "as a belated wedding present, or for an emergency." She sent the money in five dollar bills, and Norrie said nothing about it to anyone.

When the snows had melted and the ice was going from the lake she went into the nearest town on an errand for her mother-in-law and she did not come back. She went to New York instead and washed dishes there.

I asked her about her husband. "No," she said. "I knew he wouldn't care, or I couldn't have done it. But he'd been away for five months and he'd only written me four letters, and after I lost the baby he never even sent me a postcard. . . . When he was ill and lonely in London he was in love with me, but that was all gone. Things were so terribly different out there, Susan, and I was such a failure. I was better out of the way, and as we'd never had a church wedding and I was a heretic I expect he made it all right with the priest. Not that I thought about that till later. I was past minding."

Norrie smiled, the slow smile that made her look like Henry. "I've never told anyone the story of my life before," she said. "When I came back to England I still felt too raw to want to talk about it, and I knew everyone would say they'd told me so, which they hadn't. And then . . . well, I got interested in other things.

"But I've enjoyed talking about it all now. It's so long ago that it seems as if it had happened to somebody else. I don't blame myself any more, or at least it doesn't hurt. That's one of the compensations of getting old, Susan. You don't feel responsible any more for any of the things you did and thought and said when you were young. Somebody else was silly and humiliated and hurt, but it isn't you any more. Unfortunately that consolation only comes when it's too late for you to need it."

The "All clear" had gone. The clock on the mantelpiece pointed to midnight. Norrie moved round the room emptying the ashtrays and clearing the tea cups, while I watched her and thought how neat and deft she was, and how unlike Austin with his clumsy movements and his spattered waistcoat. She mistook my look.

"I suppose you can't understand why I did what I did? You've always been happy. Oh, I don't mean *now*. But you've always had people to love you and want you. When I first met Philip Etienne I felt no one wanted me. Before I met him I used to lie awake at nights listening to the rats and the creaking of the boards, and I thought of my life closing in on me like walls. I was afraid I should grow into a crusty old maid like Cousin Liza with nobody wanting me. I used to get in a panic. And of course, I was terribly easily pleased. If I hadn't gone off with Philip, I should have gone off with someone else, I expect."

Norrie lighted another cigarette. "It would never have happened," she said judicially, "if Mother had been different. When I was little, before Melissa and Henry were born, I used to adore her. She used to play games and tell us stories, Austin and me, and we loved Mary's afternoon out and coming down to the drawing-room. And then she changed so much . . . to me at any rate, though she was always devoted to Austin. After Henry came she was really quite peculiar.

"I used to wonder sometimes if something dreadful had happened to her . . . only I don't see what it could have been. I suppose it was just her health and living with Father. He could be pretty trying at times."

Before I went to sleep that night I thought of what Norrie had told me, feeling glad that I knew so much, because it made me like her even better than I had done before, far, far better than Melissa. Directly or indirectly, both their lives had been spoilt by their upbringing, but Melissa, with a different character in the beginning, had been damaged in herself so that her bitterness soured everything she touched. Norrie, on the other hand, bore no grudge to herself or anyone else, and her memory dealt kindly both with her husband who had disappointed her and the parents who had loved her so little. Like Henry, she had a nice nature.

[V]

It was the fortunes of war and the helping hand of Norrie that led me to Oxford, to the house of Aunt Catherine Lestrange.

At the beginning of 1942 my department tardily decided to evacuate itself from London, and January found me shivering in lodgings half-way up the Cowley Road, and feeling very sorry for myself. They were extremely bad lodgings from every point of view, and when I wrote to my sister-in-law I described their shortcomings in some detail.

Three days later Norrie replied, enclosing a letter in a rather spindly handwriting, signed "Your affectionate aunt, Catherine Lestrange." Aunt Catherine was in trouble. She had had a doctor billeted with her, and he was now leaving the neighbourhood. She was justifiably anxious about who might take his place, being, she said, too old now to like being over-run with strangers. "If you're still uncomfortable," wrote Norrie, "you might do worse than ask her to take you in. I think you would get on well together, and she would be pleased because she is very 'family.' I'll write to her, if you like, and suggest it."

I was somewhat chary of acquiring another relative, but over-crowded Oxford seemed to offer no other escape from the Cowley Road. I went to Aunt Catherine.

The arrangement was not tested by time, but for the six months that I lived with her it worked very well indeed. Aunt Catherine treated me from the first day as a member of the family, and because I saw so little of her the relationship remained a privilege. I was out all day, and she always breakfasted and frequently dined in her own room, for arthritis was making her progressively more crippled and she was often in pain. We met only at week-ends, and on occasional evenings when she was feeling well enough to come downstairs. When we met I always found her excellent company. She was well-read, mildly musical, and an earnest student of the *Times*, such attributes being expected from the wives and widows of elderly dons. But her real interests lay elsewhere.

Aunt Catherine was of the select band to whom gossip flows with the easy inevitability of steel splinters to a magnet. She needed only to look out of her window or down the street to see something interesting, something to be either recorded and filed for future use or placed significantly beside some fact already known to her; no detail of life passed her by. And to these gifts, exercised largely unconsciously, she added a capacious memory and a racy narrative style. But she was no purveyor of vulgar tittle-tattle. She was an Olympian, as perfect in her own sphere as the high gods and very much more discreet. She never stooped to scavenge for information, nor to trade her knowledge to the first comer as a sop to her own self-importance; neither did she make mischief through choosing her audience carelessly. She was, in short, a discriminating collector of gossip rather than a common retailer.

For more than forty years she had entertained undergraduates to tea and dons to dinner, until war and rationing and her own ill-health prevented her. I was a veritable god-send. Her best days of collecting were over. My coming could not alter that. But I was an appreciative listener, and she regarded me after a time as a fellow connoisseur, able to admire her treasures and value their best points.

When she was in the mood and had congenial company, Aunt Catherine was a relentless, though an entertaining, talker. She had a large store of good stories, some of them quaintly improper, about well-known university characters, and an even larger number of tales about her own family, of which I was an adopted member. She had been born and brought up in a leisured world, and many of these legends went back, by a kind of oral tradition, to her parents' youth or earlier still. To this day Great Aunt Selina, who shared her bed with a marmoset, and the butler who thought he was Parnell whenever the moon was full, are as real as any characters in Dickens, while her own immediate family, her parents and sister, and their intimate friends and relatives, are living people to me whenever I think of them. I know what they wore and their taste in food, and what they were like to look at, and what were their politics. I know when they were born and whom they married, and how many children they had, and I know just what Aunt Catherine thought of them and why. She was a shrewd old lady and she did not mince her words.

Of her younger sister Helena, who had been my mother-in-law, she spoke with an odd mixture of spite and affection. Nell had always been the attractive one, she said, the pretty one, the clever one at school, and it was a thousand pities that everybody had spoilt her so much, because for all her faults she used to have a very sweet nature. There was only a year between them and as girls they did everything together, but apparently Aunt Catherine had accepted the role of foil without jealousy. Nell was more gifted than she was; there was nothing more to be said.

But on one subject she was harsh. Her sister had always been secretive, and what she wished to hide remained hidden from even the most kindly probings. Like a high-class burglar defeated by a safe, the old lady felt sore, even after so many years, at this absence of candour. "Nell was sometimes most unreliable," she told me, "and she grew worse as she became older. Marriage did not seem to have at all a good effect on her in that respect.

"Our mother used always to say: 'You can lock the door against a thief, but not against a liar.' Not that she was really a *liar*, but you never knew what she might do. . . . I was most displeased when I discovered that she had been pretending to William that she was staying with me when she was not. And she did that more than once. I could never find out where she had been," Aunt Catherine added regretfully. "Not, of course, that I wanted to know if she did not wish to tell me."

Such incidents had rankled. She revenged herself by making little jabs at her sister whenever she spoke of her. She probably hardly knew that she did it.

But the famous quarrel (referred to as The Quarrel to distinguish it from the common run of domestic differences) came over nothing new or dramatic. Their friendship even survived the days when Aunt Catherine championed the runaway Norrie to her outraged parents and advanced money to Melissa for her first training at the Slade ("and much gratitude she ever showed me, though that's neither here nor there.")

Shortly after Dr Prioleau's death she went to stay at Rye with her sister and Austin, and unwisely took it on herself to ask Austin in his mother's hearing when he was going to get some work to do. With a singular absence of tact she added that she was sure his father would not have wished him to be a loafer. Mrs Prioleau flew straightway into a rage (this being something of a habit with her), accused her sister of inhumanity, and taunted her with having had no children.

"Really, Susan dear, she quite forgot herself. She was both incivil and indelicate. It was many years ago, and I think I am wiser now than I was then. If such a situation could possibly arise to-day I would ignore it. But we said things . . . It all became rather undignified in the end, I'm afraid . . . and then we had hurt each other so much that there was nothing more to be said. We never met again, though I tried to forgive her in my heart."

It was a sad little story, commonplace in all its details, but for me it had one quaint feature which seemed never to have struck either of the protagonists. Mrs Prioleau's elder daughter had run away from home, and her younger son had tried to do the same. Her younger daughter had cut herself adrift at the earliest possible moment; her cherished elder son was a nervous wreck. In different ways she had mismanaged all four of them. Yet it never occurred to her that to have children could be other than a subject for self-congratulation.

"Poor Nell!" said Aunt Catherine sadly, "she was really quite idiotic over Austin, and he was such a promising boy until that dreadful war. . . . If only she had married a different man! . . . Though indeed," she added with some surprise, "if she had married poor Rowley, Austin would not have been Austin."

"Or Henry Henry, for that matter."

But such abstruse speculation did not greatly interest her. She returned to the subject of Rowley, the handsome young man of whom Mrs Spencer had spoken, the first love of Helena Crawfurd, who jilted her or whom she jilted.

Again the old sore rankled. Helena had cried on her sister's shoulder, but she had never told her what really happened. "She talked a great deal of rubbish about sacrifice," the old lady said crossly, "and cried herself into an illness, and said her heart was broken, and then she went and married Willie Prioleau in the teeth of everybody, and poor Rowley . . ."

But at this point something happened. Jane brought in tea, or we discovered that it was time for the news, or else, as sometimes happened, Aunt Catherine simply side-tracked herself. My knowledge of Rowley is from another source, and comprises more than even she could have told me.

PART II
BEHIND THE REFLECTION

CHAPTER I

[1]

It is a common rule of civilised behaviour, though one which is not always observed, that one does not read other people's private papers while they are living; but when they are dead and can presumably be embarrassed no longer, the prohibition is not so stringent. Strictly speaking, in my case, it was sheer inquisitive prying which led me to read Mrs Prioleau's journal and her packet of love letters, but I had famous precedents and excellent excuses. There might be something in them of interest or importance to her family . . . they might be of literary or even historical value . . . they might contain, or hint at, scientific discoveries made by her husband the doctor. In short, once I had found them it was positively my duty to look them over, and even though the world benefited not a whit thereby, none the less they were interesting reading.

I discovered the bundle quite by chance in a pocket in the dressing-bag that Austin had given me. I had the lock opened and a new key fitted to it as soon as I got back to London, and then I put it into store with a trunk full of my winter clothes and forgot all about it. I did not use it for more than two years, since it was heavy and held very little, and I only used it then because my week-end case was being mended. When I began to pack I found it would hold even less than I had thought, the reason being a large pocket concealed behind the fittings and evidently designed to hold a jewel case. In it were a crayon sketch and two small photographs, a couple of scrawled dance programmes, a bundle of letters, and a small stout book, bound in heavy morocco leather, and labelled "My Journal" in florid gold copperplate. The leaves, which were of thin India paper, were nearly covered with my mother-in-law's pretty fanciful handwriting, which grew wilder and more careless as she grew older, so that I found it quite difficult to make out some of the later pages. I read to the end, partly from curiosity, and partly because she had the gift of the born writer, and was never dull, even when she was being enthusiastic about the beauties of Italy or the mysteries of first love.

The letters, all written in the same hand, covered altogether a period of some seven years before and after her marriage, from 1896 to 1902. They were love letters, written to her by someone who signed himself Rowley, and they formed a tragic commentary on the contents of the diary. They were arranged chronologically in their envelopes, and tied by a piece of ribbon which had grown draggled from being frequently tied and untied. The paper was rubbed and crumpled, as though they had been carried in pockets and handbags, and here and there the ink had run in pale blue smudges that suggested tears.

There was nothing grand about these letters. "Rowley" was rather trite as a correspondent, with a stilted style which led him to "commence" and "conclude" nearly everything, and to put a remarkably large number of commas in all his sentences. Yet in come curious way the very banality of the writing made them the more touching. He was so devoted, so confident in himself and in his Helena, ready to work for her, to wait for years if needs be, determined to make her proud of him.

"I do not deserve that you should wait for me," he wrote in his first letter the day after they became engaged, "but since you declare you are prepared to do so, I have not the courage to refuse your offer. I can only promise that I will try to be worthy of your affection." And then, only a few months later the blow came, and on the eve of sailing for India he wrote his farewell to her, wishing her luck as the wife of William Prioleau, poor dull Cousin Willie whom no one in the family had ever taken quite seriously. "Most sincerely I hope that you will be very happy with the man you have chosen, and with this hope I will disappear without reproaches from your life."

But she had not been happy, and Rowley had disappeared only for a time.

Although the style of the photographs suggested the eighteen-nineties, they were unmistakably likenesses of a younger slimmer Austin, taken perhaps twenty years ago. It was sad to think how much he had deteriorated; in those days he had been good-looking, even handsome. The crayon sketch which I found with them depicted the same young man. It was unsigned, and had lost a good deal of its clarity from rubbing, but I thought I recognised my mother-in-law's hand in the sure line and rather lush colouring. It was quite a charming piece of work and I debated whether Austin might not like to have it. Finally, I decided that it would be cruel even to show it to him. His mother had depicted him as a young Bacchus, with bright eyes and a laughing eager mouth and vine leaves in his hair, and now the most kindly imagination could pose him only as an incompetent middle-aged Silenus with a poor head for liquor.

And she, the artist, the writer of the sad little journal in that smug little book, the girl whom poor Rowley had loved for so long? She had been gifted and charming and affectionate, so that everyone who had known her then remembered her still with a warm kindliness; and the years had warped and twisted her into a malevolent yellow-faced woman, who spent her creative powers in writing virulent letters, who loved her son with a love that rotted him to the soul. Her decline was no less tragic than Austin's.

When I first read her diary there was much in it that meant nothing to me, but when I went to stay with Aunt Catherine and listened to her talking of her girlhood in Ireland, the obscurities in it gradually became clear to me. Bit by bit, like a jig-saw puzzle, the story of my mother-in-law built herself up in my mind, the pieces falling into place in ones and twos and then in whole groups, until now the pattern of her life seems clear to me in its growth and decay, and I believe I know what she was really like and why. I understand her perhaps better than anyone ever did who knew her while she lived, and she has become a single entity to me instead of a gallery of labelled portraits painted by people who saw her only from one angle. The radiant girl, the sad-eyed mother with her young children, the aloof cruel woman with the heavy face, the empty corpse so frantically mourned by Austin on that cold spring morning, are resolved into one person instead of a medley of contradictions, and even now that she is dead I still feel sorry for her. She made such a dreary mess of her life and the lives of the people who loved her best.

Those who write diaries and letters about their own feelings are probably never wholly sincere, and much of the interest of this sort of reading lies in trying to find out whether the writer was a conscious fake, presenting himself as he would like to appear, or an honest self-deceiver who really believed that he had plumbed the most subtle depths of his own personality. Mrs Prioleau posed, I think, quite without being aware of it, and where her thoughts and judgments appear trite or ordinary she was merely expressing herself in language usual to a young girl of her period and with her background. She was brought up to think and to write like that, and she did so naturally. She was not trying to impress herself or anyone else.

She wrote for two reasons, both of which she explains on the first page of her journal. It is dated June 21st, 1894, and reads:—

"To-day is my seventeenth birthday. I am beginning this journal because I am naturally of an expansive disposition, and now that Catherine is from home there is no one in whom I can confide. When we are young, older people laugh at us when we say what we think and feel, or smile because (they say) we are young and know so little about life. Sometimes when I am very happy or very miserable I cannot keep all my feelings and thoughts to myself, but I do not like to be thought foolish, so I intend to write them down in future, so that people need not know what I think unless I want them to.

"There is another reason why I am commencing this record of my life and feelings. I have always observed that older people lose touch with young ones. I know of course that it is right and proper that Mother should have different opinions on many subjects from Catherine and myself. She says that when we are her age we shall agree with her that it is unsuitable to go hatless to the lodge gates where passers-by may see us, and realise that although there is nothing *wrong* in walking down Grafton Street after tea, nice people do not do it.

"This is possibly the case, though I suppose that time alone will show. Meanwhile I want to write down what I *do really feel* now that I am seventeen, and not what other people say that I ought to feel, or am going to feel when I am seventy. I shall try to be honest with myself and not shrink from laying bare my faults and failings, and then perhaps when I am old, if I am fortunate enough to have children, I can turn to this little book, and be helped to understand them better than I otherwise would do."

Poor lady! She kept her little book, and I think she read it, for it is well-thumbed, but it certainly never helped her to understand her children, and when she turned to it, I think it was less for help than to torture herself by "remembering in adversity the happy times that are past."

Because the young Helena was interested in herself and her feelings rather than in what actually happened to her, the diary is kept in an erratic fashion. Sometimes she wrote pages at a time, and sometimes nothing for a week or more. "Twenty years from now," as she goes on to explain in that first entry, which might almost be described as a preface, "I shall probably not be interested to read that I had Miss O'Malley make me a winter costume of sky blue velours trimmed with squirrel, or that Jessie stumbled with me at Mulligan's Gap, but I shall like to know how I felt when I first wore my new dress, and if I was frightened when I felt myself fall."

Her story, as told by herself, is full of gaps, but when I stayed with Aunt Catherine I was able to fill most of them in. I never told her of the diary, or even pretended to an extraordinary interest in Henry's mother. She was of an age when the mind slips readily into the past and she needed no prompting.

Crawfurdstown, as she described it to me, was a straggling ugly little village of whitewashed cottages and an inn where the farmers used to drink on market days, the Catholic chapel, and the Church of Ireland church where the congregation was so "anti-popery" that the more forceful of its members, with the full support of the rest, twice tore down and smashed a Celtic cross erected in the churchyard by the local lord in memory of his wife.

The Crawfurds lived outside the village in a big house surrounded by a park and known as the Demesne. It has all gone now, for the lead was stripped from the roof to pay for a lawsuit, and in the Troubles some English soldiers besieged a dozen rebels in the shell of the house and it caught fire during the shooting. The timber in the park has been cut down, and the stone boundary walls are flat for most of their length, and the gate-lodge stands empty by a grass-grown track that was once the drive. Aunt Catherine had not seen it, for it was many years since she had visited Ireland, but kind friends had told her of the ruin in every detail. She said to me that she would hardly recognise it as it was now, and I think she never thought of it except as it was when she had known it as a girl.

It had been a comfortable enough place then, and the occupants, except for the servants who existed laboriously in the basement, led comfortable and leisured lives. The house was always full of friends and relations, who stayed for days or weeks or months as the fancy took them. There were picnics and dances for the young people, tea and dinner parties for their elders, and parties of a rather more solid kind for Mr Crawfurd and his cronies. The girls and their friends hunted in the winter and talked horses all the year round, and the greatest outing of the year was to the Dublin Horse Show. Sometimes the ladies were driven into Greystones and caught the train into town for a day's shopping, or Mr Crawfurd went in protestingly to attend to his business. Occasionally they went on visits to relations who lived similar lives in similar houses. It was a simple existence of which the only obligations were to be pleasant and friendly to everyone and to go to church twice on Sundays.

The Crawfurd parents, though Helena writes as though they were monsters of incomprehension, seem to have been a nice couple and devoted to their children. Before he was "saved," or, as his elder daughter put it, "before poor Father had that peculiar illness," Mr Crawfurd was apparently a genial and friendly person with simple tastes and a liking for practical jokes. The stables were at the back of the house, and with a splendid disregard for comfort, he chose his bedroom especially so that he could watch the horses and talk to the grooms while he dressed in the mornings.

Mrs Crawfurd, who was the daughter of a Dublin lawyer, was suitably attached to her husband, but believed to the end of her days that country people were savages. She painted a little, and sang, and had once been to Italy, and she tried without much encouragement to be cultured. (Aunt Catherine showed me a miniature of her in an oval frame set with brilliants, a pretty, plump woman with a fleeting likeness to Norrie.) Having little interest in horses, Mrs Crawfurd greatly disliked Mr. Crawfurd's choice of bed-chamber. She said that the room was full of flies and the smell of stables, and insisted on spraying it with eau de Cologne every night and keeping the windows shut against pollution. She also took for herself a smaller room in front of the house which she called her boudoir and furnished with Burne-Jones reproductions and small statues in imitation marble. Her husband found this vastly amusing and her daughters rather admired it. Being a forceful woman in her quiet way, as well as something of a snob, she had them both sent to boarding school in England, and later they studied painting and music with masters from Dublin. She also saw to it, when the time came, that they were duly presented at the Castle and went through the season in the proper manner.

Aunt Catherine loved to talk about every detail of their lives in those legendary years before the crash came, but over one fact she was slightly apologetic. The Crawfurds had made their money "in trade". Henry Crawfurd, my Henry's great-great grandfather, had been the original maker of "Crawfurd's Mountain Dew," and his descendants were always trying to forget it. Victorian Ireland was even more snobbish than Victorian England, and it was not always quite easy to do so. Fortunately, however, for some curious reason, it has always been more reputable to make whisky, or even beer, than pork pies or ladies' dresses. Fortunately, too, the family had been at Crawfurdstown for generations before the distillery. Mr Crawfurd was rich enough to ignore the source of his income and did no more than attend and obstruct an occasional board meeting. The family was virtually financed by the labours of a works manager whom they patronised kindly and sometimes invited to dinner at the last moment when they were a man short.

[II]

Helena had already left school when she began her diary, so that there is no record of her rather sensational manner of leaving. However, Aunt Catherine told me all about it one day, and I was interested because the affair and her comments gave such a clear foreshadowing of what she was to become. Fundamentally people's characters never change, but the way they live alters the emphasis, and they may grow lop-sided, rather as women used to do who rode too much on the old-fashioned side-saddle. Mrs Prioleau let her life pull her out of the straight so that in the end all her dangerous qualities grew and developed at the expense of the rest. But they never grew from nothing; they were there all the time.

Aunt Catherine was reminded of those distant school-days by reading a *Times* leader on education, and she told me the story of their end with the usual spice of faint humorous malice.

The two girls had not much cared for the English school which their mother had chosen for them, though Aunt Catherine minded it less, because she was older and steadier. "Nell didn't like it at all," she said, "even though she was popular with the girls and I was the dunce when it came to lessons.

"We'd both been spoilt at home, I'm afraid, and she was always indulged particularly, because she was such an amusing little girl and so pretty. She always wanted her own way, and when she was crossed she flew into a rage or sulked, though of course that happened very seldom.

"Well, she could climb like a monkey . . . she was much lighter than I was, and far better at games and riding . . . and one day one of the girls . . . Elsie Reed was her name, I think . . . dared her to climb out of the bedroom window in her nightdress and on to the roof and up the chimney-stack, and she was to collect some soot in a paper bag and bring it back to prove she had done it. Well, she did it all right, but she dropped the bag on the way, so she blacked her face with the soot instead. Poor Helena! She was always unlucky. Miss Osbourne, our head mistress (we always said she wore a wig, because her hair was such a peculiar colour and always so very neat), was passing along outside and heard the other girls laughing as she came in. And there was poor Nell with her face all black and half the front torn out of her good nightdress! A fine kettle of fish, and no mistake!!

"Helena was moved to a little bedroom next to Miss Osbourne with only a skylight in it, and she was made to wear the Robe of Repentance . . . a horrid white thing made out of a sheet . . . and a placard on her back for a week with 'I am a most immodest girl' printed on it. She was terribly angry, and nearly as angry with me as with Miss Osbourne, because she said Miss Osbourne told her I never did anything I shouldn't. Which was quite incorrect, of course, for I was just lucky and never got caught.

"A few days afterwards Miss Osbourne sent for me. She had a large bottle of sal volatile, and she always used to put it out on her table with a little glass and some water if she had to break anything unpleasant to one of her pupils, so I knew as soon as I came into the room that something was wrong. She told me that a telegram had just come from Father saying that Mother was dangerously ill and we must both go home at once, and I was to tell Helena to take off her placard and go and pack.

"I didn't need the sal volatile, but I was very much upset, needless to say. When I told Nell she gave me rather a queer look and just asked what train we were going on. I had expected her to cry and make a scene, for she was always extremely emotional, and I thought she must still be angry with me. We couldn't go before the next morning, but we were excused work, and the news went round, and everyone was very kind to us . . . even Miss Osbourne . . . and Helena grew more and more depressed. That evening she had a terrible fit of crying and shivered so much that I was quite frightened, and of course I cried too, and Mr Simmonds . . . that was the rector. No; Timmins was his name, and he had a red beard . . . came and read the Bible to us, and we were allowed to use Miss Osbourne's sitting-room.

"Then the next morning Helena looked quite pleased with herself, and Miss Watson who took us up to Euston said to me that she was afraid my sister was quite hardened. I couldn't understand it at all.

"Well, the long and the short of it was that there was nothing at all wrong with Mother, and that Helena had made up the whole thing from start to finish. All the way to Holyhead she sat looking as pleased as a cream-fed cat, with me beside her thinking we should come home to find Mother dead already and trying not to cry, and then when we were on the boat she told me. Of course if Miss Osbourne had looked carefully at the telegram she would have seen that it was only sent from Ealing or some such place, but Helena had worded it quite sensibly and I suppose she was rather upset and never thought of it.

"I can see Helena now walking beside me on the deck. She had a funny little habit of skipping when she was pleased. . . . Poor Mother always said that it was most unsuitable . . . and she was jigging up and down like a hen on a hot griddle. She had bribed a housemaid, she said, by promising her Aunt Florence's coral bracelet, to send the telegram on her day out, and wasn't it clever of her? I should never have thought of that, should I?"

There was a dull flush on Aunt Catherine's cheeks, and her voice arose at this tale of ancient wrong. "Angry! I've never been so angry in my life! If we'd been alone, I declare I should have hit her and enjoyed it! When I asked her why she had not told me before she said she was afraid I would give her away because I was so good, and that anyway she wanted to punish me. She was a queer girl, Helena! She loved having secrets, though she mostly told them to me in those days. She would keep something to herself for days, or weeks even, and then produce it when it would make a sensation . . . or not at all.

"'For goodness' sake, Helena,' I said, 'if you knew it was all an invention, what on earth made you go crying the place down for last night?'

"'Well,' she said, 'it's a funny thing, Kitty, but by that time, what with you bawling and roaring' . . . which I was not . . . 'and everyone being so kind, and Miss Osbourne waving sal volatile at us, and old Timmy talking in that silly voice of his, just as if we were in church, I began to wonder if I'd invented it or if it was true after all, and I got terribly frightened in case Mother was really dying.'

"Helena was always like that, fanciful. . . . There's some grand name for it nowadays . . . and she had a wonderful invention. I've known her make up ghost stories at school to frighten the other girls, and by the time she had finished she was as frightened as any of them, just by her own inventions. The worst of it was that she never seemed to realise that she was doing anything wrong.

"When we got home Mother was very angry and said we should go back by the very next boat, but Helena got round Father as usual. I was leaving anyway, at the end of the term, so that it was hardly worth sending me for such a short time, and Nell wheedled and cajoled him and told him how miserable she was away from home, and how terribly she would miss me next term . . . which was all true . . . and he gave in.

"But it was bad for her all the same, to be spoilt like that. She thought she could get her own way always by fair means or foul, and later when she couldn't manage it any more she was so terribly hurt. Happiness never comes dropping out of the sky, except perhaps when one is quite young, and she always thought it should do. Poor Helena!"

I went to bed that night in my shabby, comfortable bedroom, with more pieces in place in my jigsaw puzzle. I could understand now how Mrs Prioleau, who as a schoolgirl could frighten herself to tears with her own imaginings, could later on, when life was unkind, find comfort in a trunk of finery and believe herself a princess in exile by dressing in outlandish garments.

[III]

Dublin society at the end of the nineteenth century was exclusive and conservative to an extraordinary degree. To people like me, the Dublin of that period means Bernard Shaw and James Joyce and W. B. Yeats and Lady Gregory and the Abbey Theatre, all the brilliant beginnings of that cultural ferment which was to merge later into the nationalism of the Easter Rising. To the Crawfurds and their kind, these people, if they realised their existence at all, were simply a minority of cranks who behaved in varying degrees of bad taste.

For them England was the sun round which their feebler planet revolved, and Dublin meant the Castle and the Horse Show, and balls at the Vice-Regal Lodge, and a yearly round of festivities modelled on those of the London season. The wealthier among them bought their clothes in London and sent their children to be educated in England, so that they might lose the "horrible accents" which the English find so attractive. They were more loyal than the king, more British than the flag, and Protestant with an intensity only possible in a Catholic country. They were too poor and had too much native originality ever to become perfect imitations of their English models, but they tried their hardest.

Because of their unfortunate connection with "trade" in the shape of whisky, the Crawfurds had to try particularly hard. When Catherine was due to "come out" the Lord Lieutenant of the day was under suspicion of favouring Home Rule, and his court was boycotted by all the usual Castle set. Mrs Crawfurd therefore waited to present her elder daughter until the following year when he had retired from office, and she and Helena made their curtseys together. Helena was so impressed by the proceedings that she broke through her rule of not describing clothes and factual happenings in detail, and her diary gives quite a lengthy description of the event under the date of February 9th, 1897.

"I have never seen such a splendid spectacle or such a blaze of light and colour, and I never thought I should see so many beautiful women. Mother pointed out Lady Limerick to me blazing with sapphires, and the Duchess of Leinster and the Countess of Waterford; and Miss Cornwallis-West was there with her sister and a number of other ladies of rank. They all reminded me of beautiful flowers, and indeed the men were scarcely less fine in their court dress. Father says he has no idea why they should wish to be taken for admirals, and I can see what he means. All the same it looks wonderful. Their Excellencies looked very fine and stately, too; she was wearing a gown of maroon velvet and a tiara of diamonds, and he was positively *covered* in medals. I was unable to observe very closely, however, for it was something of an Ordeal, and my heart fluttered so that I was almost afraid that I might faint.

"At the same time, even though I was only one of a large number of debutantes who walked up the hall as their names were called, it was rather wonderful to think that everyone was looking at me as I made my curtsey. I suppose actresses feel like that. I flatter myself, too, that I looked well, for the cold always gives me a colour, and it was extremely cold both in the barouche and in the ante-room where we waited beforehand. Kitty, who came before me, did not look her best. She was not nervous as I was, for she is less sensitive and feels things less, but cold weather makes her very pale, and a veil and ostrich plumes in the coiffeur are not becoming to such a long face as hers. I felt very sorry for her.

"My dress is wonderful, though it is a pity we had to wear black bows on account of the Battenburg mourning. It is the thickest of thick satin with the bodice all worked over with fine silk braid and the skirt ruched with tulle at the hem, and caught up with sprays of black and white lace flowers. (N.B. It was made to my measure by Madame Fabian who comes from Bond Street!) Mother lent me her train and Catherine had Aunt Flora's. I shall wear my dress again without the train at our own ball on March 10th.

"It is always difficult, even immediately after an event, to distinguish what one *actually* felt from what one knows were the correct feelings for the occasion. I think I felt shy and proud at once . . . shy because it is an Ordeal to have so many smart and distinguished people watching one, and proud because I knew I was looking my best and had practised until I was confident both of being able to make a graceful bow and of retiring backwards from the Presence without treading on my train, which is a difficult feat! Anthony Hewitt acted as one of His Excellency's aides and he tried to catch my eye as I was coming up to the dais, but I would not look at him. He looked very handsome."

Following the presentation came the usual round of balls and parties, both private and official, culminating in the St Patrick's Day Ball on March 17th. Helena's comment on this is that it was not very exciting as there were so many girls. "However I generally got partners though Kitty was less lucky. I suggested to Anthony H. that he should ask her for another dance, but he said he would rather dance with me. It is rather difficult to accept a remark of that kind gracefully, I think.

"Willie Prioleau was there, brought by Mrs D'Olier Herbert. I danced with him once and he asked me for another, but I said I was engaged. He is a bad dancer and very stiff, and does not look as if he enjoyed himself. I think he disapproves of us all! Poor Kitty had the supper dance with him, and he made her feel *quite sick* talking about slums. Mother says that she considers this a *most unsuitable* topic of conversation for a ballroom, particularly as an accompaniment to refreshments, and I agree!"

At this same ball there was some slight trouble about Anthony Hewitt. Helena engaged herself to him for three dances, including the supper dance, and was afterwards seen by Mrs Crawfurd eating ices in his company behind a screen of palms when she should have been dancing with a certain Captain C. Mrs Crawfurd conducted her quietly to the ladies' cloakroom, and told her that she would get herself talked about if she behaved like that. Two dances in an evening and perhaps an extra were quite enough for any young man, even though he might be a second cousin.

"Of all the rubbish!" raged the diarist. "I told her that I sat down for a moment because my shoe pinched and he came up and began talking to me. I could hardly refuse to answer him, after all." Mrs Crawfurd, however, seems to have found this explanation unsatisfactory.

Helena Crawfurd kept an extremely voluble journal during her first season, but on the whole it is not very interesting, except for the light it throws on her character and surroundings. It is full of people who come and go, but the majority remain as mere names without materialising as individuals. Being confessedly interested mainly in her own reactions to them, she never sees them other than subjectively, as foils or stimuli to herself. But she herself emerges very definitely as a person, self-willed and indulged and a little vain, but warm-hearted and full of that vital charm which can be so dangerous to its possessor. At that age she was as strong and tireless as a pony, and I think the most attractive thing about her must have been her capacity for enjoyment. Everything was "lovely" and "wonderful" and "most interesting," and even when she found some function tedious, like the St Patrick's Ball, she writes as though she had managed to have a pretty good time. She even gives the impression that she enjoyed being unhappy, and she was unhappy sometimes with all the anguish of seventeen. She revelled in her "sensitive nature" and her "artistic impulses," and could comfort herself in the deepest woe by reflecting that she felt things more deeply than other people.

Her family unfortunately tended to share her view of herself. Mr Crawfurd looked on her indulgently as his "clever daughter" and paid for her music and painting lessons as he would pay for corn and the best clover hay for a promising filly, while Mrs Crawfurd, thwarted in her own mild aspirations, saw in her the fulfilment of all that she herself had wished to be. In short they spoilt her at her sister's expense.

Helena had a good soprano voice; Catherine played her accompaniments. Both girls painted flowers and landscapes, but Helena did so really well, and the family spoke of "poor Kitty's daubs". Both girls were good-looking, but most of Catherine's admirers were Helena's leavings. Helena was thoughtless and impetuous, Catherine the steadying influence, stable, matter of fact, conscientious, everything that her younger sister was not. She bore no grudge.

Rather surprisingly, and in spite of occasional quarrels, Helena was devoted to her, and gave her the fullest credit for her good qualities, though she never tried to emulate them. "I wish I were more like her," she writes after an unfortunate episode in which she had given her father's overcoat to a beggar in the mistaken assumption that he would not object. "Kitty always does the right thing. She never acts first and thinks afterwards like I do, and she is really far kinder than I am, because she has a *really* beautiful nature, while I am kind because I like to be admired, and because it makes me feel uncomfortable when other people are unhappy." Many years later, when they quarrelled, she would write and speak far otherwise about her.

[IV]

During the spring he spent in Dublin Dr William Prioleau proposed to Nell Crawfurd and she refused him. He was in his late thirties, and serious-minded with the single-track fanaticism of a humourless person with a mission. He had neither looks, money nor prospects, and he was entertained by mothers of daughters only because they thought him such a "detrimental" that no girl could possibly consider him as a husband. He was already in practice in London, but he had turned his work over to a *locum* and had come back to Dublin where he had formerly been a student to study for six months at the famous Rotunda in order to bring his own methods up to date.

He was some kind of cousin of some people who were some kind of cousin of the Crawfurds, and he drifted into their parties and excursions for no better reason than this vague cousinship. He was singularly incongruous amid this light-hearted band who met at dances, and went riding together in Phœnix Park, and sang and acted charades, and played harmless practical jokes. He was ten years older than the oldest among them, and he had not danced or ridden for years. He had no parlour tricks of any kind and his power of repartee was extremely limited. He was accepted with careless good nature as an apparently necessary evil and never realised that everyone referred to him as "Poor Cousin Willie."

Like so many bad mixers he yearned to be liked, and went to parties not because he enjoyed them, but because he hoped he might and because if he stayed away he always felt he was missing something. His childhood and student friends had long ago disappeared from Dublin, and he was far too shy to make congenial acquaintances on his own initiative. So the Crawfurd cousins took him up because they were clannish and kind and "poor William was no trouble," and when he was not too busy studying he went to their house and sat about looking faintly like a stray dog and wishing he was being more of a success. With part of his mind he knew that his relations were lighthearted and flippant, and regarded everything he was interested in (if they regarded it at all) with apathetic and irresponsible ignorance. Part of his mind disapproved of them thoroughly; but he was lonely and grateful for their casual kindliness.

He proposed to Helena after their famous walk through the Henry Street slums, an expedition which remained firmly fixed in her sister's memory. "The Dublin slums," said Aunt Catherine to me with the faint note of pride which comes into the voices of the nicest people when talking of conditions in their home town, "the Dublin slums used to be some of the worst in Europe. I hear they've pulled a lot of them down now, but some people make a slum of anything. Of course one never went near them in the ordinary way, but that day . . . I've forgotten now why it was . . . Willie and Nell and I were through the worst of them. It was a warm day in March, and I remember I had on a new pair of glacé kid shoes, and they pinched a little corn I had. We'd never intended to come there, you see. It was really most unpleasant, for everyone was in the streets, and I knew Mother would be vexed with us for coming home so late.

"There was a most peculiar smell about, which made me feel quite sick. It seemed to come out of all the doorways, and Willie said it was 'the smell of dirt,' and insisted upon going into details about it. It was really not at all nice. All the women wore shawls, and they looked so wild and abandoned, and some of them were sitting on doorways actually feeding their babies, and the little children were crawling about *doing things* in the gutters. It made us both feel dreadfully embarrassed, especially with Willie there . . . though we should have probably felt worse without him. He didn't feel that way at all, being a doctor, though he said such places were a disgrace to civilisation . . . which they were, of course.

He pointed out a dreadful old man with no nose, and a woman with a queer way of walking, and told us what they were suffering from. They were very rare diseases apparently, and he got quite excited.

"My feet were getting to feel like boiled puddings and I was terribly tired, and worried about Mother and how annoyed she would be when she knew where William had taken us. But when I said something about my shoes he said every woman in the last half mile must have been envying them. Poor Willie! I think he meant it kindly, but I was *very* cross. He was always such a tactless man. No wonder Nell . . .

"Well, when we were nearly out a terrible looking woman ran beside us with a shawl over her head, and her hair all pulled about her face, and a black eye. She had a wretched little baby wrapped in the shawl, and two poor dirty little children with sores on their faces hanging on her skirts, and no shoes to her feet, and she began begging from us. She said her husband had just beaten her and turned her out, and indeed she looked the part, the poor creature. She fastened herself on to Nell and she was moaning and crying. And 'Don't give her anything,' says Willie in a whisper, 'or we'll have a dozen of them on our heels.' He felt responsible for us, of course, and I think he was getting a little alarmed in case we should be frightened or robbed. Otherwise he would have lectured us on the children's sores or the causes of rickets. 'Oh, Willie, how could you?' says Helena. She was wearing a beautiful brooch, a little swallow made of diamonds and gold that Father had given her for her birthday and she whipped it out of the front of her dress and gave it to the woman.

"Well, there was a fine old scene then. You never saw the Dublin beggars, but when we were young they were famous. The creature was clutching on to Nell and calling on all the saints to bless her for a kind, generous, lovely lady that would never see a poor woman die of hunger, and she was kissing her hand and telling her children to kiss her hand, and Nell was going red in the face, and Willie was saying: 'There now, my good woman. That's enough. Leave the lady alone.'

"But it was no good. The whole street seemed to come at us, poor little bow-legged babies and filthy old women, and they clutched at us and told us we had kind faces and asked us for the mercy of heaven to give them a penny. There was an old woman, smelling like the whole of Guinness's Brewery, that walked by me holding out her hand right under my nose, and saying she'd remember me to the Blessed Virgin every night in her prayers. Then Nell started to cry and couldn't find her handkerchief. We got out of the crowd somehow. . . . I suppose it all took only about five minutes . . . and William found a cab and took us home. He was very good, poor Willie. He made Mother a little speech . . . I think he must have been making it up in the cab . . . saying that the fault was entirely his and that he regretted we should have been so much alarmed. Mother said that it appeared to her to have been a most unsuitable excursion, but we would say no more about it. She sincerely hoped no harm had come of it, but she supposed that he as a doctor would know what he was doing. Naturally she was afraid of us picking up typhoid or something, but we none of us did."

Helena records the excursion in her journal from her own somewhat different angle. "Yesterday W. P. took K. and me through Henry Street. It was terrible. We were surrounded by crowds of filthy smelly creatures who begged from us, and Kitty was very frightened, and I am ashamed to say that I cried. I gave my swallow brooch to a woman who begged, because it all seemed so terrible and I was so sorry for her, and now I rather wish I had not. It was so very pretty, and Father will be displeased when he finds out. I think I gave it partly because I was dreadfully sorry for her and partly because I was so ashamed of myself. I hated them for looking so ugly and poor.

"Never have I seen so much wretchedness. Even the houses looked diseased. It is melancholy to think of the depths to which their own sins and the sins of others can lower men and women made in the Image of their Creator. I could not sleep last night for thinking of the dreadful sights I had witnessed, and for shame that I cannot *love* people who are so very dirty. Also I was rather anxious in case Father should find out about the brooch and be vexed. (N.B. Most of them looked quite happy.)"

Poor Helena! She was troubled by easy tears, and she cried again the next day when William Prioleau asked her to marry him. That he did so at all was a good indication of his complete unworldliness. He was twice her age, earning perhaps three hundred a year, and unlikely, in his present practice, ever to earn much more. Solemnly, in the belief that he had found a kindred soul, he offered her a share in his drab laborious life, a home in his gaunt house on the Surrey side of the Thames. She could help him so much, he said. Helena was touched, but she was fresh from the Henry Street adventure, and she could visualise it all only too clearly. It would have taken a more romantic lover to persuade her to such a sacrifice, even if she had loved him. Her cousin William was not in the least romantic, and until he proposed to her it had never even struck her that he was a possible husband for anyone, let alone for herself. He was simply "poor Willie" who had a beard like father and wore clothes that never seemed to fit and talked about peculiar things at meals. She was badly upset by the whole business.

"I think," she writes, "that I am too sensitive to take things easily. Willie's proposal made me feel so ashamed that I wept bitterly, and had to borrow his handkerchief even after I had refused him. He said he loved me for my kind and generous heart which allowed me to be moved so deeply at the sight of suffering, and when I tried to explain he said I did myself less than justice. He is far, far better and kinder than I am, for he really *loves* healing people and helping them to keep healthy. He said that I could help him in his work and begged me to think it over. But I am sure that he is mistaken. When one is in the schoolroom it is easy enough to think of giving up the world and going to live in a slum or a leper colony, but now I realise that one needs a vocation. Willie's life, as he describes it, surrounded by squalor and tragedy, fills me with repulsion. I think I should *die* if I thought I could never climb Sugarloaf again, or ride through Sally Gap when the sun shines and the clouds are breaking like waves over the hills. My artistic nature craves for beauty, and something in me will perish if ever I have to live in ugliness. I think I could love him because he is so good, but I could *never* love his life." William seems to have been rather disappointed in Helena because she refused him, disappointed not so much on his own account, as because he believed her to be an ideal helpmate for his chosen labours. He said he would pray for her that she might change her mind, and she felt too contrite to resent his attitude. A week later he went back to London.

CHAPTER II

[I]

IN APRIL the family returned to Crawfurdstown, and Helena, at a loss for more sensational material, filled her journal during the summer with rather studied passages on the beauties of nature and her reactions to them. She is at her best writing of the trifling things that really moved her . . . parting with Mary Sullivan, the old cook, who was being pensioned off after twenty years' service, or nursing a hound puppy through distemper. "And when he could drink a little milk this morning and tried to stand I knew he would get well, and I felt as pleased as if I had just been given a present. But he looked so pathetic with his sides all fallen in and his poor wobbly legs. I wish I did not love animals so much. When they suffer one cannot explain to them or tell them that they will feel better soon if they take their medicine and stay quiet. They must feel it all so cruel and undeserved."

Anthony Hewitt, "Rowley", begins to figure in the diary early in the following autumn, mentioned casually at first. He was still in Dublin and his duties were not arduous. He came frequently to Crawfurdstown for a day's hunting or to go shooting with Mr Crawfurd, and he generally stayed the night. Like Dr Prioleau he was a remote cousin, and like him he was poor; but there the likeness ended. Rowley was a good shot, a good horseman, and excellent company. Everyone liked him, and no feelings of disapproval restrained him from liking everyone in return. He was handsome, merry, young, and he fitted in perfectly with the Crawfurds and their friends. He visited their house not because he was lonely, but because he liked sport and impromptu dances with the drawing-room carpet rolled up and the guests who could play taking it in turns to pound the piano.

Helena fell in love with him, which is not altogether surprising, for he must have been an attractive youth. During the months in Dublin three men, including her cousin Willie, had asked her to marry them, and she had had several other mild and decorous flirtations, which touched her vanity rather than her heart. She had been too much occupied with her new life to take any of them very seriously, but now for the first time she was hopelessly and completely in love, and she was very angry about it. She had been brought up in the belief that requited love was the only suitable kind that could be experienced by a nice girl of good family, and thought of it as something that was produced, as it were, when the right man pressed the button. Now she found that whether she liked it or not she was in love with Anthony Hewitt, and that he showed no sign at all of being in love with her.

"I have fallen in love," she writes in November, "fallen in love for the first time in my life, like any silly servant girl.

Anthony Hewitt cares nothing for me, and I am wounded in my deepest pride, but it is true none the less. I have no idea of how or when it began, but I think that I have really known ever since last spring at the Drawing-room when he tried to make me laugh. It is quite ridiculous, for he does not care a jot for me, and would just as soon talk to Kitty, or even to Mother. If I only thought he cared I would feel so differently about it all. I know that a young officer cannot marry on his pay, but Father will make me a settlement, and later Rowley will come in for Stranent, so that there is no need for him to take the army so seriously.

"I wish I were not so foolish about it! Kitty is bound to notice soon, and Mother too. To-day when he came I felt myself *blushing*. It is so undignified and *wrong*, even though I cannot help it."

Poor Helena suffered badly during the next month. Sometimes she was scheming to sit by Rowley at table, or to ride or walk with him, and sometimes she was being deliberately offhand with him, so that her mother reproved her for rudeness. She even descended so low as to cherish for a few hours, until her sense of humour got the better of her, the torn up scraps of a note which he had written to her father. Meanwhile Anthony Hewitt came regularly to the house and brought Mrs Crawfurd flowers and listened to Mr Crawfurd's opinions on Home Rule, and was charming and pleasant to everyone without distinction or difference.

Finally, to crown her woes, Helena decided that he was in love with Catherine, and since he was irresistible it followed naturally that Catherine must be in love with him. She derived a gloomy satisfaction from renouncing him for ever ("Of course I shall get over it. It is only in books that one dies of a decline, however earnestly one longs to be dead"), and from her altered looks, for which her mother prescribed iron tonics and burgundy.

Had Rowley been as indifferent to her as she believed, she would no doubt, as she says, have recovered from her broken heart, and death might have found her in the fullness of time a very different woman from the cranky eccentric she became. Had she not ridden her father's new hunter against orders, or ridden it more successfully, or with another escort, Rowley might never have spoken as he did. On that January day her life, and his as well, was changed by the snapping of a rotten branch.

"I am going to marry Rowley," she writes on the day after her accident. "I can hardly believe it is true. I look at my face in the glass and think that he has kissed me . . . even with that shocking black eye . . . and it seems like a dream. I woke up early this morning, and though my head felt simply dreadful, I knew that something wonderful had happened even before I was awake enough to know what it was. It seems quite *incredible* that if Meg had not bolted with me yesterday it would never have happened. I should never have known that my darling Rowley loved me, and he would never have known that I loved him. How queer to think that I who have always prided myself on my good seat should owe my life's happiness to a particularly foolish riding accident! To me at least it seems like the hand of God."

It happened like this. On the previous day Anthony Hewitt, finding himself unexpectedly at a loose end, took the train to Greystones and arrived at the Crawfurds' on the mail van just before lunch. The sisters had intended to go riding that afternoon, but Catherine, who was a shrewd young woman, developed a convenient headache and said that she preferred to rest. Mr Crawfurd had just bought a second hunter, a big chestnut with a hard mouth, which Helena was very anxious to try ("I really wanted to show off in front of R., though Father had told me she pulled too much for me to hold her on grass") and she made up her mind to ride her. When Danny the groom went to saddle her own mare he found she had a loose shoe, and Miss Helena, who had previously approached him on the subject in vain, said that she would ride Meg.

Poor Danny, who knew that he would get into trouble if anything happened, protested feebly, but he was no match for Helena's blandishments. Father was at a board meeting in Dublin, she said, and need never know, and Meg needed exercising anyway. Besides, it was not as though she was going out alone with Miss Catherine. Mr Hewitt was a grand rider, as Danny should know, and he would look after her. So the reluctant Danny saddled Meg and mounted Helena with a final plea to her to try no tricks, and to her escort to keep a good eye on her.

They turned down a grassy ride outside the Demesne gates, and nothing would do Helena but that she and Rowley must race. There were overhanging trees all along, but she gave him no time to protest. She was going to show him what a good horsewoman she was, and how well she could manage Meg. Meg, who was already chafing and fidgeting, felt the grass under her feet and was off at a gallop, which left Rowley, heavier and less well-mounted, far behind. Helena turned her head to look back at him, and at that precise moment a rabbit ran out from the wood and the mare swerved wide. A branch caught her heavily across the side of her hat.

The next thing she knew was that Catherine and the parlourmaid were taking off her clothes, while her mother was laying a vinegar compress on her forehead, with the remark that she had sent into Greystones for some steak for her eye, but it would probably come too late to be of much use. Helena's hard hat and the rottenness of the bough that struck her had saved her from more serious injury, but she was cut and bruised and had a slight concussion. Catherine and Mrs Crawfurd, to whom riding accidents were only too common, told her that she should have looked where she was going, and that she was lucky not to have been dragged. She had given them a fright, and they were rather annoyed with her in consequence.

Helena wept because she felt shaken and knew that she looked a sight, and her mother gave her sal volatile and drew the blinds. It was by Heaven's grace that it was no worse, she said severely as she left the room, and Helena must go to sleep.

The rest of the tale is best told in the diarist's own words.

"Kitty brought me in some soup and bread and butter on a tray for supper, and I was well enough to eat it, though my head ached abominably. She said I must be very happy and she was so pleased, and I said 'Why?', for I did not feel happy at all. She said: 'Rowley is half frantic with worry over you. What a way to get engaged!' I thought I must be delirious. 'Engaged!' I said. 'What are you talking about?' And then I spilt the soup in the bed and poor K. had to mop it up with a towel.

"'Yes,' she said. 'Engaged to be married. He told me you were. Only you're going to keep it private for a little while yet because he may be sent to India.' Then I spilt some more soup and she had to take it away. I asked her what on earth she was talking about, and she said the blow on my head must have upset me and I had better try to go to sleep again. But of course by this time I was far too excited and I had to know what she was talking about. She said: 'Just what I say, Nell darling. Haven't you promised Rowley to marry him? Aren't you happy? Why, I thought you were in love with him. You've been behaving so oddly ever since Christmas that I knew something would happen. And he was always coming here and listening to Father talking about politics and holding Mother's wool for her.'

" 'But I thought it was *you*,' I said, and then I began to cry because I felt so happy, and Kitty looked worried and said that I must settle down and not get excited or it would make my head worse.

"So she sponged my face with eau-de-Cologne, and kissed me, and said she was very happy if I was, and I really *must* try to go to sleep again. I tried very hard, because I wanted to be well enough to see my darling R., but my head felt as if it was full of hammers, and I still could not understand in the slightest what had happened. So I rang the bell, and this time Mother came, and brought him with her. And he kissed me very gently on the cheek, and said: 'Darling! Thank God it's no worse!' And I went to sleep holding his hand.

"That all happened yesterday. To-day I feel weak and shaken and my head still aches, and my eye is a most horrible purple colour. But deep inside of me I have a wonderful warm comfortable feeling, and as I write my heart is beating in a strange choking way, and I keep on crying and have no idea of the reason.

"What strange tricks concussion can play on one! I remember nothing between telling Rowley I would race him and waking up in bed when they were pulling off my boots. My dearest Rowley (and now I can call him so with a happy heart) tells me that after I fell I appeared to be unconscious only for a moment. He had taken his coat off and was putting it under my head when I sat up. He had had a terrible fright, and he said: 'My darling, are you hurt?', or something to that effect, and I said: 'Oh, sweetheart, do you really love me?' Which of course I would *never* have said had I been myself.

"I suppose I should be ashamed of my forwardness, even though it was quite involuntary, but I can only feel gladness. Mother and Catherine seem to have known for some time that we loved each other, but my darling Rowley, being a mere man, had no idea that I cared for him, and might even have gone to India without speaking to me, had it not been for this most blessed accident of mine. As for me, his manners to everyone arc so charming that I can perhaps be excused for my mistake.

"He tells me that after that he made me comfortable with his coat under my head and had Fox come from the lodge to help him catch Meg, and he mounted me and we rode home quietly. He says that I talked quite rationally to him (though I am not so sure!). Only he had to help me down and I stumbled a bit going up the stairs. (*Note.* He says he even loves my black eye!)."

[II]

The next few months of Helena Crawfurd's journal make melancholy reading in the light of what was to follow. Through the pages of underlinings and superlatives, and lovers' phrases made cloying now by films and popular songs, the light still shines of a fresh and delicately passionate love. All her senses seemed quickened by it, so that she saw and experienced even the smallest trifles with a perceptiveness that was almost painful.

From the starlit heights she looked on everyone with a tender compassion and the pathetic belief of all young lovers that her own love was something unique, a wonderful experience such as no one had ever known or would know. "Our love will last till death and beyond it" she wrote with the sublime confidence of her eighteen sheltered years. "It is part of ourselves now, and can never change, on earth or in heaven." She pitied Catherine because she had never been in love, and her parents because their marriage seemed to her a mere comfortable humdrum arrangement for mutual convenience.

As for her lover, he was twenty-three to her eighteen, and for all his gaiety and good looks she was his first love as he was hers. She was at once his goddess and his newest toy. "You have changed me," he wrote to her in the earliest surviving letter, "so that everything I did and was before I met you seems cheap and rotten, and I feel that I can never repay you for loving me and for promising to marry me. I feel unworthy, darling, but I will do my best, God knows." (The letter continues . . . for he had the gift of bathos . . . with the information that "Juno had six fine pups yesterday, but unfortunately four of them are females.")

The Crawfurd parents, much as they liked the young man, were not overjoyed at the turn affairs had taken. Anthony Hewitt was an orphan, and until the death of a youngish uncle, from whom he would inherit a small estate in County Waterford, he had very little means beyond a lieutenant's pay. By army standards he was certainly too young to marry, and his foreign service was still to come. He and Helena talked light-heartedly of a long engagement and their elders shook their heads.

The elders were right. Helena soon began to show signs of strain, and counted all time wasted that was not spent in the company of her Rowley. Her father suggested to the young man that he should leave the army, and offered him a post in the distillery which would have enabled them to be married almost at once. But Rowley loved his profession as well as his future bride, and he was a snob to boot. He refused politely and quite firmly. Mr Crawfurd then offered to make Helena an allowance additional to her marriage settlement, so that they would not have to wait too long; but Rowley, whose charm covered a core of shrewd common sense, refused this also, pointing out that if an officer married at the age of twenty-three his army career was virtually ruined. In vain Helena implored him to change his mind. He loved her dearly, but he was a soldier first. His letter, written in answer to her persuasions, is a variation in the classic theme, "I could not love thee dear so much."

"My dearest (he wrote),

"I was grieved to receive your letter and to know that my decision had hurt you, but perhaps I did not explain properly. It is not a good thing for an officer's career for him to marry before he is twenty-five at least, and then only if he or his wife has money, which you would have. As you know, I shall probably be sent to India soon, and may be stationed somewhere where you cannot join me, which would be a disappointment to both of us, especially as Colonel T. will say that it is my fault for marrying too young, and will do nothing to help. But if we wait for another two years, I shall probably be in a better station, and since your Father is so generous, regarding money, we ought to be able to marry then.

"I want to make a success, and for you to be able to be proud of me, but I do not think you would be so proud of me if I was put on half-pay later on, or if I resigned from the Army, and took the position in Messrs Crawfurds that your Father has so kindly offered to me. I want to Serve my Country, and I should feel unworthy of you if I failed in my duty as a soldier. And so, even though I want you for my wife more than anything else on earth, I still feel compelled to postpone our marriage.

"You say that when you are away from me you feel as empty as an empty cup. It is a strange thing to say, but I understand, I think, although I could not express myself so well, of course. But I am not quitting Ireland yet, perhaps for a long period, and I cannot bear to reflect that I am causing you to be miserable, by acting the way that I consider is right.

"Perhaps I should never have permitted you to become engaged to me, but I was so afraid that another man might win you while I was away, so I dared not wait. If you feel, after thinking it over, that it is too great a sacrifice for you to be engaged to me for two years, I shall never blame you.

Your devoted,

Rowley."

Helena's reaction was a long tirade in her journal against the soulless brutality of colonels, and of Rowley's colonel in particular. Then she bowed her head. If Rowley said that they must wait for two years, then she would wait, and wait uncomplainingly. "A woman's love," she wrote, "is everything in the world to her, but with a man love should come second to his career, and there can be no real happiness in a marriage to which his career has been sacrificed. I think I should have despised R. if he had given up the Army for my sake, even though I dread the thought of waiting for such a long time. Besides he looks so wonderful in his uniform." It must surely have taken all the charm of the uniform, not to mention the wearer, to bring her to such a frame of mind.

After Rowley had refused Mr Crawfurd's offers of help, Helena's parents made a half-hearted attempt to break the engagement, but she made herself and everyone else so unhappy at the suggestion that they gave way. He would be leaving Dublin quite shortly, and they probably hoped the separation would succeed where their own efforts had failed.

("But she would have been far better off with him than with William," said Aunt Catherine to me, "even sweeping the floors of Crawfurds' warehouse . . . though for goodness' sake don't tell Henry that I said so. Poor William was devoted to her, but he was such a *dismal* man.")

Poor William, however, was not only dismal; he was pertinacious as well. Quite firmly he ignored the existence of Anthony Hewitt and wrote Helena long cousinly letters from England, to which she occasionally replied, because she was good-natured and had a ready pen which she liked using. He told her that her letters made a difference to his whole life. He knew that she had a beautiful disposition at heart. Helena giggled over them with her sister, but was of course a little flattered. It is much pleasanter, after all, to be the inspiration of a career than a threatened handicap to it.

[III]

In the spring Mrs Crawfurd took her daughters abroad in order to improve their minds, and Mr Crawfurd, unfortunately as it turned out, stayed at home. He was not a traveller. Ireland was good enough for him and he had only ventured twice in his life as far as London, once on his honeymoon and once on business; but his wife, with memories of a girlhood trip to Italy, was determined that her children should not miss this experience. Helena, for whom the journey meant several months of complete separation from Rowley, was divided in her mind, and even offered to stay at home to keep her father company, an unselfishness which deceived nobody. Lovesick daughters were not very much in Mr Crawfurd's line, and Mrs Crawfurd thought briskly that a change would do her good. She went.

The ladies stayed first in Paris. They were reasonably intelligent tourists. They read their guide books; they went to the right places at the right times, and they believed what they were told. They visited the Louvre and Notre Dame and Versailles and all the other famous spectacles; they sat through two performances of classical drama at the Comédie Française, and went several times to the opera. On Sundays they attended the English Church of St George and found it 'very popish'.

Now that she had new interests Helena began to revive, and she enjoyed sight-seeing and shopping and staying in hotels with an almost normal gusto. She and Catherine read French together conscientiously and invented funny stories about the old lady who fed fish to the cats across the road, and the pale young man from round the corner, who was with a different lady every time they saw him. They went shopping, and bought new spring costumes out of the travelling money that their father had given them, and they filled a trunk with souvenirs and presents for their relations and friends. Their mother spent much of her time sitting in the hotel lounge with ears pricked for comments on her handsome daughters, and was extremely put out when a swarthy gentleman translated his admiration into practice by trying to talk to Catherine.

From Paris they went to Rome, and from Rome to Florence and Venice. A small spirit stove went with them on their travels, so that the girls should never run the risk of drinking unboiled water, and their mother drank wine with her meals for the same reason. They had introductions in Rome, and were offered an audience with the Pope (which Mrs Crawfurd firmly refused), and a count, unfortunately rather elderly, wished to pay his addresses to Catherine. Helena congratulated herself without much conviction on the fact that no one noticed her in Italy because she was dark. It was enough for her, she declared, that her dearest R. should think her beautiful. The beginning of May found them on the shores of Lake Como with two extra trunks, a smattering of Italian, and the pleasant feeling that they had become really cosmopolitan.

During these crowded eight weeks Helena corresponded regularly with Anthony Hewitt. For a little while new sights and impressions might thrust him from her mind, so that she forgot to recall: "On such a day at this time, he and I were doing this or that together", and then she was happy with the innocent receptiveness of her mother and Catherine. But whenever she thought of him his image and the remembered happiness of shared hours stood between her and present pleasure, and she missed him always more as the weeks went by.

"It is said," she writes in her journal, "that the loss of a limb is not very painful at the time, but that later when the numbness is past, the severed nerves ache beyond endurance. Thank God, my dearest R. is cut off from me for only a little while longer, for each day the pain of separation is more bitter, and each day the beautiful and romantic scenes by which we are surrounded lose more of their charm.

"I cannot believe that he suffers from our separation quite as I do, for he is partly *consoled* by his profession, but I cherish his dear letters in which he writes that he misses me so very much. I cannot bear to think that soon he may be half the world removed from me and exposed to all the perils and hardships of a soldier's life on the burning soil of India."

They were at Como when the blow fell. It came in the shape of a letter from Mr Crawfurd to his wife informing her that he had "found God", and the results of his discovery appeared so alarming that his family took the next train for home. I never heard the exact details of what happened or why, for it was not an age in which parents confided in their children, and neither of his daughters ever knew the whole story. The most important fact as far as they were concerned was that they left Ireland as heiresses and returned as paupers.

During their absence their father had, quite inexplicably, fallen under the sway of a religious revivalist, a certain Mr Rogers, and had become convinced of the sinfulness of alcohol and of wealth which came from supplying alcohol to others. With the exception of a few shares he owned the whole of his distillery, and he had sold everything outright to a combine which planned to forward the cause of temperance by installing up-to-date plant to increase the output. And this was not all. According to his new mentor, the proceeds of the sale were "blood money". With unintentional irony he handed the whole of them to a society which provided pensions for gentlewomen in reduced circumstances. Mr Crawfurd was usually a dilatory man when dealing with his business, but his conversion had fired him with new enthusiasm, and on this occasion he worked quickly. When his family arrived home he had only the house at Crawfurdstown left, and some four thousand pounds in gilt-edged securities.

Aunt Catherine when she told me the sad story, shook her head over "poor Father's peculiar illness", and implied that he had become temporarily deranged, but from other remarks that she let fall it seems likely that he was no more insane than most other people who act first and think afterwards. He had always been given to schemes, but native laziness and his wife's good sense had kept him hitherto within bounds. Had he not been "converted" in her absence by an individual of single purpose and considerable drive he would never have indulged in his sudden and inconvenient burst of philanthropy. "Crawfurd's Mountain Dew" would have continued to keep the Crawfurd family in comfort; Helena would have married her Rowley; and . . . I should never have married Henry Prioleau because he would never have been born. It has often amused me to think how much I owe (not to mention Henry) to the unknown Mr Rogers.

News travels fast among the members of a big family. When Mrs Crawfurd and her girls arrived home the aunts and uncles and cousins and friends were already calling and writing letters of sympathy in full strength. The gist of most of their remarks was unhelpful. According to their temperaments they assured Mrs Crawfurd that she could manage splendidly, or that they had no idea how she could manage at all, or that if only they had known earlier . . . but of course this was what came of gallivanting on the continent. An invalid aunt who quarrelled with all her paid companions offered a kind home to one of the girls, and a brood of good-natured cousins, who were always considered to be rather dirty, invited them all to share their tumbledown house.

The most effective help came, rather surprisingly, from the despised William Prioleau. For over a year and without much encouragement he had been writing persistently to Helena. Now he came over to Ireland. With remarkable efficiency, for he had always seemed quite incapable of managing such small details as his own clothes and leisure time, he sorted out the tangle, interviewed the family of business, who was old and muddled, raised a mortgage on the house, arranged for the sale of a couple of farms, and, a final triumph, induced the society which provided pensions for indigent gentlewomen to return a modicum of its spoil. There could be no more continental junketings or pleasant winters in Dublin, but with care and a reduced staff they could just manage to live on in their house.

The rigours of Mr Crawfurd's conversion passed surprisingly rapidly, and he began to talk about starting a pedigree pig farm, which was probably more in his line than religious fervour. However, no one gave him much encouragement, so he took up gardening instead.

It was Helena who was most affected by the family poverty, for there could be no question now of jointures and allowances. She and Rowley must marry on hope or not at all. He wrote from Chester as soon as the news reached him, saying that he would give up the army and that they could be married at once if she wished.

It is a long letter, much of the kind that one might expect from a rather expensive young man trying to act for the best in face of a difficult situation. He is very sorry for Helena, and, as is understandable, a little sorry also for himself. It is of course quite out of the question now that he should remain in the service, for even as a bachelor he can only just manage on his pay. However, he has thought that matter over and she is not to despair. "We might be able to rent a small farm", he writes, "in some locality where the hunting is reasonably good, and I am confident that we could make a living. With your love to help me I am willing to work hard, even though, as you are aware, I am not accustomed to the life." Here follow vague and optimistic calculations on the finance of the proposed enterprise, and he ends by saying that he will hand his resignation to the Colonel as soon as possible. "Even my chosen career is not too great a sacrifice to offer to you, my dearest."

Helena received this letter on the day that William Prioleau arrived in Dublin, and although the cry of ruin had been raised a fortnight ago its full implications touched her now for the first time.

"I read his dear letter", she wrote. "I read and read it again, but I *cannot* . . . no, I *cannot* . . . accept his sacrifice. When I read once more that other letter" (presumably the one written in reply to the suggestion that he should leave the army and go into the family business) "I realise to the fullest extent the magnanimity of his offer. He would give up *everything* for me, even the profession of his choice. It is wonderful to be loved so greatly and so unselfishly, but I cannot allow him to take a step for which, later on, he might blame me *bitterly*. No. I will live and die unmarried and in poverty, rather than harm him whom I love more than life itself."

When Helena wrote this and more in the same vein she was undeniably posing, striking an attitude to herself as some protection against the harshness of reality, and perhaps there is some suggestion of pose also, or at least of pipe-dream, in the letter which inspired these lofty sentiments. In his heart of hearts Anthony Hewitt must have known that he was not cut out to be a small farmer, and that Helena was equally unsuitable for a farmer's wife. He was prepared to sacrifice his career for her, but he was not prepared, even for her peace of mind, to deny that it was a sacrifice.

The following day found her shaken into sincerity. She had lain awake most of the night, and even the brightness of daylight did nothing to dispel the sombre gloom of three o'clock in the morning. This was the first inescapable situation of her happy life, the first problem for which wheedling and tantrums offered no possible solution. She was overwhelmed. Her tears fell on the thin, fine paper of her journal, and the yellowing leaf is smudged where she brushed them away.

"I have never been so miserable before. I feel trapped. I want him so much. When I think of the years without him, living like a pauper in the corner of our house, getting old alone and unloved. No. I want to marry him at any cost, at any risk. . . .

"Oh, I am so selfish. I think only of myself, never of him nor of poor, dear mother and K. And I cannot *bear* the thought of being an old maid like poor Miss Kittery or Aunt Loo, queer and dingy and cross. Last night when I said my prayers it was like knocking my head against a stone wall. Oh God have mercy on me! I should like to die. Whatever I do I shall wish I had done the other.

"I would work myself to death for him if it were any good. I want him, not money. Oh, I wish I knew what I ought to do. I could hate Father for what he has done to us . . . hate . . . *hate.* Oh how I wish I were dead."

Poor girl! She was in a cleft stick from which there was no escape. Gone now were the visions of immortal and immutable love, untouched by time or the hardness of fate. In a calmer moment she adds with pathetic shrewdness: "He loves me as I am, but I think he might love me less later when I began to lose my looks and he realised how much he had given up for my sake and began to wonder if it had really been worth while, and that would break my heart. I am afraid that we were neither of us brought up to be very *useful* except in certain ways."

She did not answer his letter at once. For a week she hesitated and wept, and lay awake at nights, and filled her diary with heartburnings and lamentations. Her mother, worried and bitter, scoffed at the notion of farming, and Catherine, though inclined to approval, was too level-headed to give unqualified support to the suggestion. Their farming neighbours were either peasants living always on the meagre verge of ruin, or country gentlemen who rode and fished and shot and left the real work to their bailiffs. Perhaps they might manage. Perhaps Rowley's Uncle Lucas might die and leave them Stranent. . . . Perhaps . . . Perhaps . . . How could she live without him? How could she forgive herself for spoiling his life when he might be a general one day if she gave him up?

Rowley wrote again telling her that he had spoken to his Colonel, and his letter crossed one from her breaking off the engagement. For another week she waited, hardly believing what she had done, still hoping for the nightmare to break. She was physically sick now from worry and unhappiness, but she mentions the fact this time without complacency. Catherine and her mother had too much else on their minds to press her to burgundy and tonics. Finally on the Monday morning a telegram came from Rowley. He was resigning his commission at once, and would be with her next week.

But there had been too much hesitation, too much talk of sacrifice. Helena's nerve was gone, and in the house was William Prioleau and he was still in love with her. She is so incoherent at this point that it is impossible to know what happened between them, whether he asked her once more to marry him, or whether she actually offered to do so if he still wanted her. Her one wish seems to have been to put herself irretrievably out of the reach of temptation, out of reach of Anthony Hewitt whose life she must spoil. She must have given some rather different explanation to William for her very sudden change of mind, but whatever it was it evidently satisfied him.

"William is wonderfully happy, and I hope that I may find happiness too in making him a good wife. He is very kind to me. We pray together. It is like a haven after the storm of doubts, and my mind is at rest in a kind of numb peace, as though I was too deadened ever to suffer again. Dearest Rowley, and still dearest though no longer mine. I must not think of what he is feeling. But it is best so. By marrying William I put myself forever from his heart, and in time he will forget. I try to hope that he will do so soon."

"Of course," said her sister, "he caught her on the rebound. I begged her to wait a little while, and Father and Mother too, for even then there was no question of their not being able to support us. I have no idea of what she said to them, but she talked a lot of nonsense to me about doing it for Rowley's sake and finding her happiness through service. It sounded more like taking the veil than getting married. But she thought she believed what she was saying, and she talked herself into getting married to Willie, and he, poor fool, was afraid she might change her mind, and he couldn't have the wedding too soon, though a blind man could see it would never work."

And so it was that Helena Crawfurd married William Prioleau on a hot August morning in the ugly little church in Crawfurdstown. All the relations came to the wedding from charitable or uncharitable motives, and the heroine played her part with pale-cheeked composure. The general opinion, less crudely expressed, was that under the circumstances Nell was probably quite wise to take what she could get. William (whose stock had risen considerably since the vital affair of the Distillery) was a clever fellow after all, and steady, and lots of girls preferred older men, and it wasn't the gay dogs that made the best husbands. Romantic people prophesied an awful ending for poor Rowley, who was believed to have been after her money.

He sent her a fitted dressing bag, but this was not displayed with the other presents.

CHAPTER III

[I]

DURING THE FIRST summer of the war, by an odd coincidence, I spent an evening in the house where my mother-in-law had lived out the long years of her married life and Henry and his elder brother and sisters had passed their childhood. I had been asked to give a series of talks on New Zealand, and I was speaking that evening to the business girls for whom the house now served as an hostel.

It was a fine evening in summer; the last light crept over the walls of sandbags screening the windows, competing faintly with the electric bulb that hung from the middle of the ceiling in an imitation marble bowl, and in with the warm smutty London air came the smell of railway smoke and river water. Now and again a tug hooted, and every few minutes I had to stop talking while a train thundered over the bridge behind the house. No one else seemed to mind these trains because they were used to them, and I noticed later on that they talked and laughed through the noise, but to me it was simply deafening.

Some months later it happened that I mentioned the incident to my sister-in-law Norrie and she told me that I had been in their old home. Thamesbridge Hostel, wasn't it? Yes, that would be it. You got quite used to the trains if you lived there . . . except when you couldn't sleep. Then they became annoying. Mother had minded them a good deal. Had I noticed the lovely iron gates, or the fanlight over the door, or the beautiful curve of the stairs, and did everything still smell damp?

I wished I had taken more notice of the house at the time. As it was I carried away only a vague impression of high elegant rooms with shabby plaster mouldings and worn parquet floors, of rows of curtained cubicles that reminded me of my school, and a dark old kitchen fitted with new electric stoves. They had done their best with it, said the warden who took me round, but it was not really suitable. It was scheduled for demolition in 1945, and they had bought the remainder of the lease only a couple of years before the war, so that it was not worth doing more than the minimum. There was bad dry rot and they had dreadful trouble with the rats coming up from the river, and sometimes she wondered about the drains. But of course as it was so cheap they could afford to charge the girls very little, and it was splendidly central . . .

buses outside the door and Charing Cross underground just across the bridge.

Later on when I became interested in my mother-in-law I wandered down one afternoon to look at the house by daylight. It had sunk further to decay since my last visit. A bomb had evidently fallen somewhere in the rear, for tiles were loose on the roof, a jagged crack ran downwards from the eaves parting the bricks, and the windows were boarded. Weeds were sprouting sparsely on the piles of sandbags and a painted wooden board on a stake read "A.R.P. Wardens' Post." The iron gates were gone, part of the wall was down, and the space between it and the house was trampled earth half covered by a static water tank. Over the baffle wall against the door I could just see the fanlight of which Norrie had spoken. Its centre was a fluted plaster shell with delicate curves and the first floor window above repeated the motif.

It must have been a fine house in its time, and a pretty house too, with its wide doorway and rows of symmetrical windows. The tank covered what must once have been a tiny lawn, and the stanchions of window boxes still protruded from the sooty walls, and round the corner at the back peered a discouraged tree that might once have been a lilac. A hundred years ago, before the railway bridge bestrode the garden in the rear and the buses went thundering past the door, it could have been a pleasant dwelling place, but when the Prioleaus lived there its pleasantness must already have been a thing long past, and no bright curtains nor flowers nor singing birds in cages could have restored its cleanliness and peace.

On one side of the house a little alley slunk along the embankment of the railway bridge into a tangle of sheds and rubbish by the river's edge, and from it I could see the rear of the house. Its gaunt symmetry was marred by a low outbuilding of yellowish glazed brick that joined it at right-angles. Its windows, like the others on the ground floor, were heavily barred, and two of them were protected with sandbags. A side-door led from it into the alley. At one time it must have been the surgery.

The garden, little better than a back-yard, was a dreary litter of bricks and slates and nameless rubbish, the smaller debris of the raids, and sheds and storehouses divided it from the river. They were old and smoke-grimed like everything else, and looked as though they had been there for many years and would not stand for much longer. When the house was built its grounds must have run down to the unpolluted Thames, to a landing-stage maybe and a little boat. But the railway had come there before Dr Prioleau, and the grimy shadow of bridge and embankment was already turning the old mansion and its neighbourhood into a slum.

I pitied that bride who came fresh from her Irish home with its trees and clean sunshine to live there with an unloved husband, who believed that she could help him with his work, and who loved her deeply in his own dry fashion. And I pitied him too, who had so deluded himself over her as to believe that his house and his work could really make her happy.

They came there after the honeymoon, Dr Prioleau and his bride. Helena's diary is silent over the marriage and the first weeks of settling in, but she must have done her best to make the place gay. She bought fresh curtains, and William gave her new window-boxes of scarlet geraniums, and she fixed up an aviary in a little room built for a powder closet. She had a man to dig up the yard in the hopes of turning it into a garden, and she was full of plans for the papering and painting that would have to be done when the spring came.

Her sister, who visited them in the autumn, did not like her new brother-in-law any better than when he was merely her cousin. Grudgingly she admitted that Helena had done her best with the horrible house and that she seemed to be happy there, but she suspected that she was on the defensive, making the best of a rather confined and lonely life.

William was so kind, she said, and she had always wanted to live in London.

But when Catherine went home she must have been lonely indeed. Her husband's practice was entirely working-class, so that they had no friends among their patients, and when he was busy, which he always was, he did not feel the need for personal contacts outside his work and his home. Nor did he realise how much she missed them, coming from a life which had been so comfortably full of trivial gaieties. Once with much discussion and preparation he took his wife and sister-in-law to the theatre, but as he dozed through most of the performance his presence hardly added to their enjoyment. Afterwards he explained apologetically that he did not greatly care for theatres. They seemed such a waste of time.

"He was such a bore, poor man," said Aunt Catherine, and after all these years there was still a hint of malice in her voice. "No young girl wants her husband to entertain her with stories about other people's gastric ulcers, or to be told how lucky she is to have a roof over her head when she's been alone in the house for a week. The trouble with William was that he had the poor on the brain."

Indeed, Helena Prioleau's life seems to have been a curiously empty one. She was interested in the frills of housekeeping, in planning decorations and arranging rooms, but she was not in the least domesticated and had no need to be so. The cook did the housekeeping and shopping as she had done in the past and Mary Fox was a competent house-parlourmaid.

Her husband hoped that she would help him in his surgery and keep his books for him, and the idea pleased her until she tried it. Then the old disgust came back to her, the disgust that she had felt that day in Henry Street, a hatred of herself and the poor creatures whom she was supposed to be helping. She would be brutal to patients then, and afterwards full of remorseful kindness that was almost as hurtful as brutality.

"Of course they smell," said William. "So would you if you had only one set of clothes and no water in the house. For goodness sake, my dear, try not to notice it. You should try a peppermint." But she could not reach such heights of detachment. She was never asked to do more than hand instruments or hold a bowl of water, but she performed her tasks with averted head, or grew panic-stricken lest she should vomit. In a little while he gave up asking her to help him.

She had equally little aptitude for book-keeping, although she tried hard to master it, and she had an unfortunate habit of drawing faces in the margins when she found herself in difficulties and was trying to concentrate. William's protests hurt her feelings without curing her. Finally he took the books back into his own hands.

Day after day, evening after evening, young Mrs Prioleau sat alone in her drawing-room, trying to turn spare-time hobbies into full-time occupation. She strummed on the piano and sang a little; she played with her birds, and arranged and rearranged the flowers that the smoke wilted in a day. She read a good deal, and did sewing and some painting, but although Dr Prioleau did his best to appreciate her performances he was really not much interested in them. The trains thundered by on the bridge behind, and on the road in front omnibuses and carriages passed in a stream, and the shipping flowed up and down with the rise and fall of the tides; yet among all this noise and bustle she was as solitary as though she lived in the deepest country. She was expecting a baby in June, and suffered from giddy attacks which made her afraid to go out alone. Sometimes Mary walked with her as far as the Embankment, and occasionally they went to Whiteleys to gaze at clothes that she could not afford to buy and had no opportunity to wear. Otherwise she stayed in the house.

She began to keep her diary again, but now it was not a safety valve for high spirits but a refuge from loneliness. She made up stories about the people who passed in the streets, as she had done with her sister in Paris, but they were drab folk for imagination to feed on, charwomen, labourers, harassed mothers of families, occasionally a clergyman.

She blamed her dreariness on the coming baby. "I feel so heavy, in mind as well as in body. The spring is here again, but it seems stagnant, as though there were no freshness in it. The flowers in the window-boxes are simply *choked* with soot and dust, and I feel as if the soot and dust were lying on me too and suffocating me. There is a kind of fog in my brain, so that everything appears to be dim and dull and I cannot concentrate my mind. Today I attempted a sketch looking northwards from the window of the attic. The river was radiantly beautiful with a silver sheen suffused with all the tints of a dove's feathers, and the sky almost like lavender. But although I could see it as colours on a palette, I could not feel *really* interested. (Poor Coleridge felt the same, I remember, though I forget what he says.) When I showed the result to William he said: 'Very pretty my dear. We must get it framed. Do you know where my slippers are?' I miss K. so much over my pictures.

"I suppose I shall feel better when the baby is born. W. is so loving and kind when I feel unwell that I am ashamed of my complainings. . . .

". . . Yesterday night I cried because I felt that I was making him such a *dreary* wife, but he said that I was all that he wanted, and that he was *inexpressibly* happy to know that I was at home waiting for him, and that the thought of me strengthened him in all his work. God helping me, I will try to do better."

She did try too, but by upbringing and nature she was undisciplined, and she was hopelessly indolent over doing anything that she disliked. Again and again she took herself to task and vowed to do better. Again and again she slid into the dreary lethargy that was partly physical and partly the result of boredom and loneliness.

"Poor William!" she writes. "I try so hard to be what he wants me to be, and I fail at every turn. I was never intended for a ministering angel, and I told him so before we were married. He is gentle and good over my failure, but I know that he feels it. I will try to do better after baby has come."

Mrs Crawfurd came over to her daughter at the beginning of June, and at the end of the month Norrie was born. She was called Leonora Florence after her two grandmothers, and everyone concerned, including her father, thought her the most magnificent baby in creation.

"Now that we have a child, my love," said William to his wife, "I feel at last that you are really my own, and that nothing can take you from me." Though the sight of her agony tore his heart, he had attended her in her confinement, and it was between his hands that his child came from her. She was touched by his devotion and pride, and for a little while she mistook her gratitude for love.

Helena was almost happy during the six months that she nursed her baby. Her life was utterly uneventful, but she was fully occupied, and although she spent the greater part of her days alone with the child and the two servants, she was free for the first time since her marriage from the hopeless feeling of inadequacy. She was doing what William wanted, and doing it well, and Norrie was a fat contented baby who throve vastly.

But it did not last. Winter brought epidemics of scarlet fever and diphtheria, and in the poor houses behind them many children died. Dr Prioleau imposed an absolute quarantine on his wife and baby, and they were confined indoors for three weeks, lest even in the open air infection might touch them. He himself refused to go near the child, and changed his outer clothes in the surgery before entering the house. He was worked to exhaustion, often staying out all night and coming home weary and irritable to snatch a hurried breakfast before attending patients in the surgery. For the first time since she had known him he was too tired to talk to Helena even about his work.

It was a hard winter. Pipes froze and burst so that they could not light the kitchen range; the river flooded the cellars when the thaw came. Norrie was teething; she screamed incessantly and lost weight. Helena was run down and sorry for herself, and took little comfort from William, who told her that she had much to bc thankful for, and that if she could see what he had to look at daily she would be on her knees thanking God for her blessings. The epidemic seemed to have turned him from an affectionate husband and father into a remote and rather forbidding stranger. The little love she had for him shrivelled.

She went to Ireland for a month in April with Mary and the baby. It was a long-promised visit, and the original arrangement had been that William should take a *locum*, and go with her for part of the time at least. But there was too much for him to do. The long, cold spring had brought much sickness to the neighbourhood, and he was tired beyond wishing to go away.

She found the family fortunes miraculously revived, though it seems probable that her father was living on capital. Everyone came to see her and to admire the baby, and life was again as she had known it, a gentle round of tea parties and friendly visits and little trips to Dublin. Once again she was given burgundy to drink and switched eggs in milk because she was thin, and the long rides with Catherine in the spring sunshine brought back her appetite and colour. It was like old times . . . too like old times. She dreaded the prospect of returning to London.

"Time makes the thought of most things more tolerable, but now I no longer find this to be so. The longer I am away from the place I should now consider as my home, the more I *dread* the thought of returning. I think of the gloom of our house, sunless, wrapped in smoke and river mists, with its big rooms cold and empty and echoing. I think of the loneliness, the ugly people in the streets, in the horrible houses behind us. I feel that I *cannot* face it again. And then I think of poor William who needs me, and I know that I must."

At no time has there been any mention in her journal of Anthony Hewitt, though she must have thought often and sadly of him through the dreary winter that was past, and the return to her old home, where she had been happy with him for that brief spring, must have resharpened her memories. But she was married to William Prioleau, and hers was a generation of faithful wives. If she hankered for the old love in her heart she did not allow herself the luxury of hankering on paper.

Her month in Ireland lengthened into six weeks, and then very sadly she said goodbye, and went back . . . to a tired, nervy husband and a London already simmering in the first heat of a sultry summer. "I feel," she wrote on the night before her return, "as if I were going back to prison." And then as an afterthought: "Poor William! I will try to be better to him."

In August Helena received a letter from Anthony Hewitt written from chambers in Half Moon Street.

"Dear Cousin Helena (for I hope we may still call cousin after this long time!) You will, I am sure, be surprised to learn that I am in London. I am here for a few days on my way to Ireland, and I should be extremely glad to visit you and William if you would care to see me.

"An accident has terminated my army career, and I have been through a good deal since my departure from my native country two years ago. I dread meeting my old friends again, but I feel that you are too kind to be horrified, and if I can see you I may find myself encouraged to encounter other people who used to know me. You will find me very changed,

I fear. Six months ago I lost an eye and an arm in a shooting accident, and the fever which followed has injured my health considerably. I give you this information because, if we meet, I do not wish you to be unduly shocked.

"If you and William are at home and feel that you are able to see me, perhaps you will be kind enough to decide on a time convenient to you both, and inform me. My only engagement is tomorrow morning, with my dentist.

"With kind regards to you and your husband,

Your affectionate Cousin,

Anthony Gower Hewitt."

"I cannot bear to see him," wrote Helena, "but William says that it is our duty to be kind to him. He does not realise . . . and how can I explain? . . . that I am in a sense *responsible* for all that has happened to poor, poor Rowley. He only knows that naturally I am shocked to hear of his trouble. I wish I had burnt his letter and said nothing to W. But it would have been too unkind to ignore it, and besides it arrived at breakfast. Oh, why did it have to happen? W. says that we must have mince for dinner, so that poor R. may not feel awkward eating with one hand. He is so very thoughtful for anyone in trouble."

Rowley was duly invited to dinner for the following day. He looked pale and distinguished and ten years older, and he was very quiet. Helena spent a miserable evening trying not to notice his empty sleeve or the black patch over his eye. She felt sick from nerves and the food stuck in her throat. She forced it down, "because it would never have done to have shown how wretched I felt to see him so *tragically* altered."

William, on the other hand, was at his best, as he always was with anyone in trouble, and although he was practically a teetotaller he plied his guest with whisky and drank some himself. Anthony Hewitt's face showed a little colour as the evening progressed and his voice became more animated. He talked about India and about himself, speaking of his accident with a matter-of-fact stoicism which pinched at Helena's heart. Once he had started to talk it seemed as if he could not stop. Evidently he was very lonely. When at last he said goodbye William pressed him to use the house as his own while he remained in London, and he said that he would certainly come back. It was wonderful, he said, to find old friends who had not altered in the least. When Helena held out her hand to him he kissed it.

"And then I knew that I still loved him. The whole evening we had been like strangers. I had been wondering how I had ever cared for him so much, and feeling dead inside and yet thankful because all the past seemed no more than a poor, silly ghost. I wonder if he remembered. I ought to tell William that he must not come again . . . only it would look foolish, and it would hurt them both, and he is going away so soon.

"I am a *fool* to feel like this! I am a respectable married woman with a good husband and a dear little daughter, and in a few days I shall feel quite myself again."

On the day after Rowley's visit a messenger arrived bringing a handsome green parrot in a cage and a note for Helena thanking her for a most pleasant evening. He hoped, he said, that Pluto would prove a suitable addition to the aviary, and would remind her of the donor whom she used to accuse of talking too much. "The resemblance might be more complete," he added with a twist of self-pity, "only that all parrots seem to possess the usual number of eyes and limbs."

Helena was more than doubtful as to the propriety of receiving gifts from her former fiancé, but William, who was out when the parrot arrived and preoccupied when it was shown to him, said simply that it was kind of poor Anthony and he was glad she was pleased. She tore up the letter, but she quotes from it in her journal. "I try not to think I was *wrong*" she writes, referring to the broken engagement, "but I feel so *very* much to blame. I pray night and morning that God will give him resignation and comfort, and that my peace of mind may be restored, so that I may do my duty to my husband and to darling Norrie with a quiet and contented heart."

Rowley came to dinner once more, on the night before he left for Ireland, and Helena deliberately put on a frock she disliked and brushed the wave out of her hair to punish herself because she wanted so much to dress up for him. She promised herself "to behave like a respectable matron," and during dinner she hardly spoke to or looked at the visitor.

Just as they were finishing coffee in the drawing-room, William was unexpectedly called out to a confinement. "When he had gone we just sat still, and the air seemed to grow hot and heavy, and the silence was tight and unbearable as it is before thunder. I asked R. if he would have some more coffee, and I poured it out very slowly and carefully, and when I passed it to him he thanked me and put it down without drinking, and I poured more coffee for myself, slowly and carefully, and sipped it without looking at him. And the silence was like strings stretched to breaking point. I kept on saying to myself 'William-Norrie, William-Norrie,' as a sort of charm, and counting the roses on the carpet. And I knew he was going to say what he should never say and I should never listen to.

"'Look at me, Nell!' he said, and I had to look up. He looked like William sometimes does, only with W. it always makes me feel uncomfortable. 'You know I love you still,' he said. 'May I kiss you again, just once?' All the love scenes of all the novels I have ever read come between me and those minutes, so that already I hardly know what really happened except that we were like two thirsty people drinking. 'Oh, Nell!' he said, 'What have we thrown away?' Then I told him that he must go, that we had both behaved most *wickedly* and that we must never see each other again, and he laughed and said that he had certainly intended to behave like a gentleman, but he was very glad he had not. He said life owed him something after what he had suffered. I have never heard him speak like that before. He sounded so bitter and rough that I fear he is changed in more than looks. But I love him now far more than ever I did. I think I would give him my own eyes if I could. I feel so remorseful and sorry.

"I put my fingers to my ears so that I should not hear what he said, and I was shaking so that I could hear my heels tapping on the floor. I went on saying 'Go away! Go away! Please go away!' But I knew all the time that I wanted him to stay. And then he said, 'I am sorry, Helena. I ought to have known how to behave. Goodbye.'

"I shall never forget how he looked as he went. I feel so wretchedly unhappy. I want to go to him and beg his pardon for being so unkind. But I was trying to do right. He should have remembered that I am William's wife now and must behave as such . . . it is so *unfair* that I should have to make him so miserable, so cruelly unfair. . . .

"August 21st. R. called this afternoon when I thought he was half way to Dublin. He said that he had come to apologise for last night, and he stayed until Mary and Baby were due back from their walk. I am still dazed. We must both have been mad. Heaven knows that we neither of us intended to do as we did. I should have refused to see him when he asked for me, but I had no strength. We have done wrong, so *terribly* wrong that I should be on my knees praying God for His forgiveness, but I feel that I could only thank Him. Later on I may feel guilty and ashamed, but now I can only feel glad. R. has gone, and goodness knows when or how we shall meet again, but even this seems nothing . . ."

Helena never touches more plainly than this on the physical aspect of her love. The product of her class and generation, there were things that she could not bring herself to formulate on paper, even for her own reading, and these omissions in her writing make the love between her and Rowley seem at the same time unreal and curiously touching. According to their own code they were committing the worst of all possible sins, and they knew it well; yet even while they planned and plotted and deceived the unsuspecting William their relationship preserved a strange innocence indefinably above the level of mere intrigue.

She lived in the present, and if she foresaw danger she did not let her mind dwell upon it. Rowley was less certain than Helena of the complete rightness of their conduct, but hers was the stronger character and she would overrule his misgivings. With the ruthless logic of a child she justified to herself the betrayal of her husband so completely that in a little while her conscience hardly felt a twinge. William had so much; the career he loved, two eyes and two arms, a wife and child, a home and security. And Rowley had nothing. She was doing no harm to William since William knew nothing about it. She was even doing good to him because she was so much happier than she had ever been before that he could not fail to notice it. She began to sing again and to work at her painting, and she made him two shirts for his birthday and a pair of embroidered slippers. With renewed enthusiasm she set herself to please him, washing bottles in the surgery, working once more at the hated books, even helping him with dressings when he was particularly busy. The poor man was delighted that she seemed to be really contented at last.

It was very easy to cuckold William, even from across the Irish Sea. Rowley obtained some sort of small post, a sinecure at the toy court, which gave him occupation and a minute salary supplemented by the uncle whose heir he was. He came over to London sometimes in charge of special mail, and no one seemed to notice how many days he stayed.

Catherine was married by this time, and he and Helena invented the game of "visiting Kitty". The procedure was simple. Whenever Rowley crossed to England, Helena, notified of his advent by an irrelevant postcard from an apocryphal Mary or Florence, told William that she would like to stay with Kitty for a few days. He was generally quite agreeable to her going, and when she returned he invariably commented on the good that the little change had done her.

It was ironical that Helena's happiness as the wife of Dr Prioleau should be brought about by an attachment which could only wreck her marriage with him, but the fact remains that for a short time she was very happy indeed. The journal even returns to the style and manner of her girlhood, written no longer because she was lonely and had no one to talk to, but because happiness welled from her and must find an outlet. A gay vitality illumines this record of her days; the trivial happiness of her small world. Norrie, over a year old and beginning to talk, was a constant amusement to her, and the antics of Pluto the parrot were hardly less entertaining. She read too, and went to art shows and concerts whenever she had the time. The twilight oppression that had clouded the first years of her marriage was lifted. Between the brief days that she spent with her lover she could live richly on memory and anticipation.

Over and over again she must examine this splendid new possession of her love for Rowley. "It is like a wonderful new toy that I must always be touching and playing with in my mind to make sure that I have it still and that it is real. I try to look at it from all sides, from all *possible* sides, and always it is new and unexpected and beautiful, like a precious jewel.

"It has so many sides, as well as the obvious one. It has liking and understanding and pity and gratitude and the sharing of tastes, and perhaps most of all, the feeling of being *at home*. When I am with my dearest R. I feel as free as though I were with another self, as if we were one soul, instead of two. Surely there can be no sin where we feel like this!

"Once I thought that I loved William or that I could grow to love him, because he loves me so dearly and I can give him so little in return that I must pity him, and he is such a good man and so kind when I have been sick that I cannot regard him except with admiration and gratitude. But he does not understand me and I fear that I shall never understand him, or be really at ease with him. Until my dearest R. returned to me, I did not know what I was missing, but he has taught me what love can be like, and now . . ."

For ten months Helena continued loving Rowley and being kind to William and looking no further into the future than her next "visit" to the unsuspecting Catherine.

CHAPTER IV

THE END came in the March of 1899, when Helena discovered that she was going to have a child. There could be no doubt who was the father, for William had had influenza earlier in the year, and had not even slept in her room since because he still coughed at nights and did not wish to disturb her.

Helena was almost wild with anxiety. She knew that in his own dry way her husband loved and trusted her, and she still seems to have been fond of him, as well as a little afraid. She was shocked to think of how deeply she might hurt him. From the ruins of her fool's paradise she wrote frantically to Rowley in Ireland. What ought she to do? His reply, which she did not preserve, seems to have been unhelpful.

The problem had a practical side just as serious as the emotional. Neither she nor Rowley had any money, and if there were a scandal he would probably lose his post and have nothing to live on except the doubtful bounty of Uncle Lucas. And she herself would be hardly in better plight if William divorced her. She would have only what he or her family might chose to allow her, and the best she could hope from her parents would be a pained and unforgiving pardon. Separately or together she and her lover would be ruined by exposure.

Always fertile and without discipline, Helena's imagination ran riot now in depicting every possible and impossible catastrophe. Piteously she wrote that she knew that God was punishing her, and wished with an earnest futility, as she had wished three years ago, that she might die. She remained alive.

Out of the incoherent pages of her diary one incident stands out, the sordid and pathetic solution of her problem. "I know now what I must do," she writes, and on the next day: "I have done it. . . .

"By my own act I know now how a bad woman must feel before she becomes hardened to vice. I am ashamed and humiliated beyond language. It was cheap and horrible . . . doing my hair like that and putting on my best night-dress, and *visiting* him to find out if he was comfortable. . . . And telling him I love him when I never can, when I wanted to be *sick* because it was him and not R. If I were brave I would face it out and beg his pardon, but I dare not, and if I did, it would do nothing but harm to us all. I feel unclean, as though a thousand baths would never make me clean again. A prostitute is good and honourable beside me. And poor W. was so *pleased*. It seemed as though this made it even worse . . ."

Austin was born in December, rather earlier than anyone but his mother had expected him. Mrs Crawfurd was ill, and Catherine was abroad with her husband, so Cousin Liza came to keep house for the family. I never discovered her other name, but she was a Prioleau connection, a kind of universal aunt with the auntly privilege of an awkward tongue.

She remarked how very unlike any of William's family the new baby was; she supposed that he inherited the birthmark on his neck from his mother's side and was most interested to know whether any of Helena's relations had a similar peculiarity. She thought it odd that Helena should stay so frequently with Catherine when Catherine came so seldom to her. Did William agree? She added that Helena would find she had less time for gallivanting now that she had two children. Helena was grateful to her for her help, and still more grateful to the relative whose illness removed her once more to Ireland.

Things seem to have begun to go wrong from the time Austin was born. When Norrie was born there had been no counter attractions, but Helena found Austin as much a nuisance as a pleasure. She had not seen Rowley for months, and a second baby would make it even more difficult for her to do so in the future. She was most anxious to avoid the tie of nursing him, but when she told William hopefully that nursing made her feel faint, he replied brusquely that it was all nerves, and that she would feel better if she took more exercise. As her husband and her doctor, he would be seriously annoyed if she gave it up.

On a sudden inspiration Helena suggested that she should take Austin to Oxford to visit Catherine, but William refused to allow her to travel alone in case she should turn faint in the train, so she had to "visit Kitty" quite genuinely in the end, and take Norrie and Mary Fox with her. She had a pleasant enough fortnight, but it was not quite what she had wanted.

At William's suggestion however, Rowley was asked to be Austin's godfather, and in the future this gave colour to his visiting the Prioleau's house when he came to London. He generally came in the afternoons, and with any luck William was out for part or all of his visit. Helena lived for these rare meetings as she had lived before Austin's birth for her stolen days.

But the fine bloom was already off their love, worn by time and the friction of constant planning. They were too seriously involved to take their relationship lightly, as a transient bond to be broken when it became irksome. Though romance had fled, they needed each other more as time went on.

"You are the only person," he wrote to her, "with whom I feel natural and at ease. With everyone else I am conscious of my mutilations, and know that they regard me with sympathy or curiosity or distaste. But with you I never think of them at all, except to wish for your sake that I was whole."

And Helena needed him as much. She needed him as a clock needs winding; she said that when he was too long away she felt like a clock beginning to run down. In a little while she was beginning to think seriously of leaving William.

She had begun to hate him almost from the night that she deceived him with her calculated love-making. The feeling grew slowly, pushing up into her consciousness as a sprouting seed breaks through to the air, and her diary records the change more faithfully perhaps than she realised. The pity and admiration disappear. No longer is he "poor dear William" and "so good and kind"; she makes no more vows that she will try to be worthy of him. Instead she girds at him faintly but with increasing spite, noting his matter-of-fact obtuseness, resenting his devotion to his work, his lack of interest in her painting. He has no idea of companionship, she writes bitterly, and all he wants is a female echo of himself, a housekeeper and a mother with no thoughts beyond the four walls of their home.

Finally, after another difference of opinion over "the books", in which she first omitted and later faked an entry, she realised fully how she felt about him. Characteristically too, and almost in the same sentence, she was justifying and blaming herself.

"When my dearest R. and I met again after so long, and found that we still loved each other, I thought that W. and I could still go on as we were, that my life could hold the two of them. But now I know that William is *robbing* Rowley and me, robbing him even of his son. He deserves, yes *deserves* to be lied to. He stole me when I was a girl, full of ideals and noble ambitions, and played on my good-nature and my vanity until I married him. He took me when I belonged to Rowley, and now he is paying for it!

"Sometimes when I watch him in the evenings, dozing in his chair, with his breath coming in little puffs through his teeth, I long to waken him and tell him the truth, to shout it in his ear so that he understands everything. Then perhaps he would stop calling me his dear child, and thinking to himself that he has tamed me at last.

"What would he do, I wonder; turn me out of the house, pray over me? I almost wish he would find out, so that we should be forced to put an end to this dismal living on crumbs. Today, when I have heard and seen nothing of R. for so long, half of me feels capable of any cruelty to William, of murder even. But with the other half of me, I know that I am to blame and *only* I. I know that I hate him because I have deceived him, and his trust in mc rcproaches me every time I see him with Baby. He has given me everything that he is capable of giving . . . so much that I do not want and so little that I do . . . and I am a swindler who has taken everything and given him nothing in return. Part of me knows that I hate him because he is far, far too good for me."

The climax was reached one day about eighteen months after Austin's birth, when Rowley paid one of his periodic visits to the house. On an impulse Helena begged him to take her away with him. She would leave Norrie, Austin; she would make every sacrifice of comfort or reputation. Anything was better than the life she was leading, the constant separation, the furtive meetings. And he refused.

Rowley's character does not at any time emerge very clearly from Helena's records, because she loved him too much and was with him too little to be able ever to see him otherwise than completely subjectively. He may have been less capable than she was of loving passionately and making sacrifices over long years, or he may have been genuinely afraid for her sake to take the final compromising step. She does not attempt to gauge his motives in refusing.

"He was right I know, because if I went away with him we should not have enough money to live on. But oh, how sad, how *tragic* it is that we should have to pay so dearly for my mistake! If he had not lost his arm we might still go away somewhere and try farming or breaking horses. I want so little now . . . only to be with him and away from this horrible house and this atmosphere of lies and pretence. But now . . . we must wait he says, until Uncle Lucas dies . . . twenty years hence perhaps when we are both old and tired and burnt out, or until William dies and I can marry him without scandal. I try not to feel that if he were in my place and I in his I would choose differently. In a way, I am braver now than I was once."

This is the nearest Helena ever comes to condemning Rowley. To the end she was uncritically loyal to him as she never had been to her husband; and the end was approaching now, the real end, to which their final parting years later was only an unimportant epilogue, at least for her.

There was nothing dramatic about it. William did not discover the truth and forbid Rowley the house, nor did Rowley fall in love with someone else. Helena and he did not even weary of each other or part by mutual consent. Quite simply, the practical circumstances of her daily life were too much for her and love went the way of her painting and her music. She had no time.

Mary Fox married Bob Spencer, her policeman, and the girl who took her place as nurse housemaid was young and inexperienced. Austin was a sickly baby with a tendency to croup, aggravated no doubt by the dampness of the house and the smoke-laden mists of the river, and his mother did not dare leave him. Norrie was five now, a bright and noticing child, who adored her mother and was always with her. When Rowley came to the house it was difficult to avoid her attentions, and it was seldom now that they were alone together for more than a few minutes at a time.

"He has no place in my life any more," Helena wrote with infinite sadness. "He came today on Betty's day out, and all the time we had the children with us, and after tea I had to bath them and put them to bed. He read to Norrie and saw Baby in his bath and then we had half an hour before W. came in and it was time for dinner. And we had nothing to say to each other, we who used to find the day too short. I was tired, and my mind was full of *worry* about half a dozen things . . . Norrie's cough and Baby's teeth, and what we should have for tomorrow's dinner.

"If it had been *his* house and *his* children (for Baby is his only in one way, since he sees him so very little) we could have talked it all over together. But I felt that he *could* not be really interested, although he tried to make out that he was. We talked of his crossing, and of Dublin, and of K. and Father and Mother, polite talk that could have been listened to by *anyone*. And then he went away, and I felt almost glad. It was as if there was a great wall between us, or we were just talking with our lips while our real selves were dumb. I think he must have felt it too, for he went sooner than was necessary.

"If only we could be away alone together, I know it would all be as it used to be in the beginning, but that is impossible. The children and the house and the surgery accounts, my whole life with William, occupy me against my will, and there is no real room for him any more in my life."

There was no room for him any more, yet she could not let him go entirely. Rowley gave up coming over to England, ostensibly because his work no longer permitted it, and she did not press him to come; but they still corresponded, and his letters, jealously guarded from William, were an assurance that he loved her still. But she does not seem to have kept them, and they can have given her little real comfort. The years were long, and letters are but a frail link between people whose lives have ceased to touch, except where one of them has the genius of a Sévigny.

Yet Helena still hoped. An illogical optimism assured her still that Rowley's Uncle Lucas could not be perverse enough to live out his normal span, and she indulged herself, as on drugs, on stories of what they would do when he died. They would go to Paris together, she and Rowley, and to Italy and to Spain, and to Egypt and India; they would be rich and courted, with the whole world at their feet. Rowley would be made an ambassador perhaps, or even a viceroy. They would live happily ever afterwards.

William and the children, even Austin, were expunged from these fantasies; the scandal of divorce was overlooked, and poor Rowley had two arms and two eyes again, or suffered no longer because of his disability. Uncle Lucas's modest fortune, a small place and sufficient income to keep it going, swelled to enormous proportions, and when it came to them it would enable them to live in more luxury than Helena had known even in the comfortable days of her girlhood.

These fairy-tale intrusions into what is otherwise a commonplace and scrappy little chronicle, are pathetic for all their silliness, and not less so because Helena knew exactly what she was doing and why.

"It helps me to pretend like this, to escape from the drabness of real life, and eternal coughs and colds, and flannel shirts, and stews for dinner. I suppose that it is rather like taking to drink, except that it costs nothing and does nobody any harm."

When she was feeling depressed she was quite truthful with herself, admitting that her poor love affair had little chance of rebirth, save in imagination; but normally she carried her optimism to an extraordinary degree, even to making a kind of trousseau for her elopement. Until Melissa was born in 1904 she busied herself intermittently on making the charming clothes and hats that Austin and I found packed away so carefully in the boxes in the attic. She made them in the evenings, working on them quite calmly in front of William, and telling him about charity bazaars when he asked her what she was doing. William sat on one side of the hearth, reading or dozing, and she sat on the other, sewing dresses that she hoped to wear in the house of another man, and smiling secretly to think what would happen if she told her husband what she was doing. It was a piece with her saying so often how much Austin resembled his father, a sort of warped and futile revenge on the unfortunate William for continuing to be her lawful husband and her sole means of support.

Uncle Lucas died unexpectedly in 1908, just six months too late to benefit Helena. Rowley came to tell her that they need wait no longer, and she sent him away. She was six months pregnant with Henry.

Her marital relations with William, on which she touches but little, must have been sordid indeed during these years. It was one of the many tragedies between them that he loved her always in his awkward austere fashion, while at best she never felt more for him than a grateful tolerance. He must have been a thoroughly uncomfortable husband. His puritan turn of mind made him ashamed of his passion, and after he had lain with her he would pray to be delivered from the sin of lust.

Helena, for all her secretiveness, was a bad actress who found it nearly impossible to disguise her feelings however much she might lie as to their cause. "He would feel less badly if I could pretend better," she wrote in the early days. "But he *embarrasses* me quite dreadfully, and I *do not like* to be prayed over."

After Austin was born she refused to share her husband's room at all on the grounds that he disturbed her when he went out at night to urgent cases. She does not record his reactions.

Norrie told me that she remembered, as a schoolgirl, being wakened by hearing her father go into her mother's room, and then their voices going on and on, and hers rising finally on a wail of hysteria. "Oh, William, be kind! Don't touch me! For God's sake, leave me alone!" Then silence.

Norrie was just old enough to realise that other girls' parents generally shared bedrooms, but the significance of what she had heard did not strike her then, though she was very frightened because she thought they were quarrelling. Another time after her father had left her mother's bedroom she heard her crying.

Henry and Melissa must have been conceived in these or similar crises of shame and frustration, but although Helena is frequently spiteful about William in her diary she is silent here. She must have felt the scenes too badly even to write about them. The first intimation of the impending birth of Melissa runs: "I am feeling terribly sick. The baby is due in March." And Henry's advent is heralded in almost identical words.

Helena always felt sick and languid during her pregnancies, and from her point of view the unfortunate Uncle Lucas could hardly have chosen a worse time to die. When Rowley brought her the news she was overpowered by it rather than pleased. It had happened too late.

Almost laconically she records their meeting after so long, and their parting, this time a final one.

"R. called yesterday. I had not seen him for nearly five years, and he gave me no warning. It was a dreadful shock. The children were out with Betty, and I was resting on my bed when Cook announced him. I told her that I was not able to see him, for I could not bear that he should see me looking so ugly, but he walked right past her and into my room. He was carrying a big bunch of roses, and as soon as I saw his face I knew that his Uncle must be dead and that we were free. And I knew at the same time that I could never be free again.

"It is curious how, when one is deciding something of vital importance, one listens to one's own voice as though another person were speaking. I had thought so long of this day, imagining it and planning, but I never thought that it would come when I was lying on my bed in such a *condition*, and wearing a *crimson flannel* dressing gown. It should have been a wonderful surprise to see Rowley after so long, but under these circumstances it was a *shock* rather than a pleasure, and everything was so different from the way I had imagined it that it seemed quite unreal.

"I told R. that I could not go to him, because I was expecting another baby, and because I could not bring myself to leave the children. I could hear myself saying all this in a small pedantic voice, and I could speak slowly, without hurrying, picking my words. It was a strange and horrible sensation, almost as though another person were speaking with my voice while I listened.

"Part of me knew that this was the end, and that I was deliberately throwing away my only happiness, and the other part was glad because this was the real end at last, and now, in a sense, I should be free, because I should never again be faced with the choice of giving up my darling Austin.

"I watched R.'s face while I was speaking, and he looked as though he could not believe me. Then he asked: 'Do you really mean this?' and I said: 'I do.' 'Well,' he answered, 'I suppose there is nothing more to be said,' and I said: 'Nothing.' He kissed me then on my cheek and walked out of the room, still holding the roses. It seemed as if somebody else was watching him go, and not I.

"Perhaps it is like this when someone you have loved very dearly dies after a long, painful and hopeless sickness. We are dead now to each other, and later I know that I shall feel this most dreadfully, and reproach myself for having played him false again as I did when we were both young. But just now I can feel only a sort of numbed relief, because it is all over at last and I shall never be torn in pieces again."

It was over indeed. Anthony Hewitt seems to have made some further efforts to see Helena, but for once her mind was made up. She was probably feeling too unwell for drama. She would not see him when he called, and she burnt his letters without reading them.

"Because it is not worth it any more. It is old and stale now instead of fresh and lovely, and I am too tired to drag myself up by the roots.

"If R. would come and *fetch* me away *forcibly*, things might be different, but I know he will never do that because his mind, like mine, is divided. He would have to make sacrifices of reputation, friends, and perhaps money (even if W. would divorce me), and he does not love me enough any longer. As for me I would face anything else, but I *cannot* bring myself to say good-bye to my babies.

"Besides, to leave W. now, in my present condition, would be both undignified and ridiculous, and when the child is born . . ."

So Helena Prioleau stayed in Kennington Road, and Rowley went back alone to Ireland. He married a girl there whom he had known for years, and had several children. I do not know if he was happy or not, but I hope he was. Aunt Catherine once mentioned him casually as having grown enormously fat.

Henry, my husband, was born prematurely, and Mrs Prioleau nearly died. She was so ill that her parents were sent for and her sister came up from Oxford to be with her and look after the children. When she recovered, the last of her youth was gone. She was only thirty, but she looked a middle-aged woman.

"She should never have had another child," Aunt Catherine said, "especially with things as they were." Her voice tailed away while she reflected in modest silence on the separate bedrooms which Helena and William had occupied for so long. "She said," she added, pursuing her train of thought aloud, "that it was because he had to be out so much at nights, but I'm afraid there was more to it than that." She shook her head. "I never did care for beards." Poor Dr Prioleau may have had many virtues, but they had not endeared him to his sister-in-law.

Between the birth of her youngest child and 1916 when Austin joined the army, Mrs Prioleau's journal is interesting only for the light which it throws on her own deterioration. The long-drawn misery of the break with Anthony Hewitt had left her exhausted in spirit so that for a time she accepted her lot with a quiescence that seemed almost contentment. Poor William thought so, and in his gratitude became so worried at the dull life she was leading that he took her to Bournemouth for a fortnight and gave her a subscription to Mudie's library.

"He tries very hard when he remembers," she wrote laconically.

This passivity did not deceive her sister, though she attributed the change, quite wrongly, to the birth of poor Henry. Helena, she declared, with an unwonted departure from elegance, was quiet because she had thrown up the sponge.

Mrs Prioleau lost all hope, even the dreams with which she had consoled herself for so long. Her sparkle had gone, and her love of pretty clothes, and the dingy house became more dingy as she surrendered without a fight to the eroding grime of London. The flowers wilted from the window-boxes and the aviary was empty, and dust lay thick in the upper room that she had once called her studio. Only Pluto remained, a strident survival, shouting and banging on the bars of his cage in the nursery. She gave up going out of the house, at first because it was too much of an effort, and later because she had lost the habit. "It is part of me now," she wrote, "like the shell of a snail, so that I cannot imagine what it would be like to live elsewhere. I neither like nor dislike it. As we grow older I suppose that all our feelings become less intense, for I do not care about anything now as deeply as I once did. I can even tolerate William."

The only person whom she really loved was Austin, who was handsome and docile and sunny of temper. "And the odd thing was," said Norrie to me, "that Mother used always to say that he was the image of his father, and no one else could see it at all."

This likeness worried Helena increasingly, for Austin became more and more like Rowley as he grew up, and sometimes she was afraid that, even thus belatedly, William might guess the truth.

The respectable Protestant God of her parents, the drab and high-principled God of William to whom he prayed night and morning, had never been very real to her except when she was unhappy, and then He became the God of Wrath, punishing her for her sins. Now, as the years passed and she saw in her eldest son the image of her half-forgotten lover, she began to side with this avenging deity, and to take upon herself, in His name, the offices of a moral censor. It was, I think, quite an unconscious effort at self-protection, for the pages of her journal ring with the authentic notes of righteous indignation. Her later habits in connection with letter-writing rose perfectly logically from this same state of mind.

But there was another aspect in her relationship with her husband, an aspect which completely contradicted her feelings of guilt. "It amuses me," she writes, "to praise Austin to him and to hear him say that he is a good boy and congratulate him when he does well at school. It is a strange exciting sort of feeling, like inviting someone to sit with you on a barrel of gunpowder while you play with matches that are hidden in your pocket." To the day of his death she continued to take her revenge on William thus for all the real and fancied ills which she had suffered at his hands; but it must have been an empty pleasure. William ignored her. She was no more to him than his housekeeper, and not a good one at that. He treated her generally with a distant courtesy. If she tried to quarrel with him he went out or locked himself in his study.

She became increasingly quarrelsome with time, like an animal made savage with captivity, and when she was in the mood she attacked whoever was at hand, venting in a storm of temper her irritated nerves and the frustrations and disappointments of her married life.

She must have enjoyed these quarrels, for she records them all in their wealth of trivial detail when she writes of nothing else. The fine handwriting stabs viciously on the thin paper, and invective rolls from her pen.

There was, for instance, the unfortunate occasion when Jessie the housemaid, while doing the washing, inadvertently lost one of the doctor's socks down the wash-pipe of the sink where it lodged in the drain. Mrs Prioleau discovered it upon a morning when she happened to be feeling exceptionally militant. " 'Jessie,' I said, 'in all my life I have never seen so destructive a girl. Nothing, positively *nothing* is sacred from your filthy paws. No wonder your mother sent you out to service, you slut! I suppose she could not bear with you even in her own hovel! And this is a decent house, I would have you know. You are no better than a thief! You rob me of all my household goods by breaking and losing them.' And the creature had the *impertinence* to answer me back! She said that she had never been called a thief and would not put up with it. I replied that if she had not been told the truth before she should know it now." And so on through pages. Finally the injured Jessie burst into tears and retired to her room, emerging later to give in her notice.

Two days later came the reconciliation, following the inevitable pattern of these scenes. "I found poor Jessie this morning with tears in her eyes, and when I asked her, she admitted that she was sorry to be going. She had always been happy here, she said, but she could not stay anywhere where she was called dishonest. I am sure that I never called her any such thing" (Mrs Prioleau evidently did not always reread what she had written), "but perhaps I spoke hastily as

I do when vexed. As the sock was not lost or seriously damaged (beyond being slightly shrunk), and we did not in the end have to send for the plumber, I felt that I might demean myself, without loss of dignity, to apologise for having hurt her feelings. The poor girl was so *overjoyed* . . . she was, I think, afraid to go home to her mother . . . that she burst out crying, and, as she appeared to have no handkerchief, I lent her mine and held her hand until she had dried her tears. I felt so sorry for her that I nearly cried too. In the end I gave her my blue satin blouse, and she said that she would always remember my goodness."

This attack on Jessie, more comic than most in its origin, is a pattern for many similar ones, all of an appalling triviality; a tear in Norrie's stocking, the loss of Henry's penknife (though this might be thought mainly to affect Henry), the cellar light left on by Melissa were all equally causes for battle. First came the furious attack, goading the victim to return abuse for abuse, and then the reconciliation, tearfully dramatic and obviously enjoyable to the principal party. Quite astonishingly, the technique always worked. She must have kept her charm even when her gaiety had gone. It was only when she was in the mood to quarrel that Mrs Prioleau really seems to have become alive during those years. At other times, as when Henry ran away to sea and she had really some provocation, she defeated all the fears of the criminal by taking no notice whatever of the crime.

The diary breaks off for no apparent reason just before Austin was sent to the front. The last words are scrawled nearly illegibly in pencil. "If he is killed, then I will die too, and perhaps join him. I dare not think . . . I am so terrified, God will punish me for what I did by taking him from me. Heaven knows I tried to do my duty once, before life grew so hard. Heaven knows I love him as once I loved poor R. I cannot face such punishment . . ."

She never had to. The retribution that came to her was too subtle for her to recognise it, and maybe at the last it overtook her unaware. That is one of the many things that I can never know.

CHAPTER V

WHEN I WAS a very little girl at home in Auckland we had for neighbour a certain Mrs Mogeridge, whom I remember as a vast putty-coloured woman with a dreary manner and a habit of turning up unexpectedly when we were having a particularly good time and spoiling everything with her gloom and grumblings. Her favourite saying was: "Laugh in the morning, cry before night," and somehow after her visits something always seemed to go wrong. My father christened her "The Portent".

In those far-off days, Mrs Mogeridge or no, I generally cried from sheer excitement before the end of the mildest parties, and even now, when tears have long ceased to be part of my routine, I recall her sometimes almost with apprehension. So very often things have gone wrong when I was enjoying myself particularly.

On a certain night in August, 1942, however, Mrs Mogeridge was far from my mind. I was in London again, back with Norrie after my six months in Oxford, and Austin was up from Suffolk on forty-eight hours' leave. I had just had news that Henry had been mentioned in despatches, and I had an idea that he might soon be due for some leave. The evenings were still light, so that generally the raids began late and ended early. I invited Austin and Norrie out to dinner, as a kind of celebration.

We had a good dinner, for war-time; and we were all in the mood to enjoy ourselves. I was feeling proud and happy because of Henry, and Norrie, who is temperamental in an unobtrusive way, was happy for the same reason, or for no reason in particular. As for Austin, he asked no more of life than to eat good meals with people who liked him and would listen to his stories.

It was a stuffy evening, with streets and buildings still throwing out the stored-up heat of the day, and after dinner we stayed for a long time in St James's Park watching the strolling couples and the birds on the ponds. The ducks, who never go to bed at the normal hour, were bathing gleefully, and Austin produced a piece of bread out of his pocket and amused himself feeding them. He was, as he had always been, completely unselfconscious in the company of animals, and he insisted on sharing his bread with us so that we too could feed the ducks. They were very greedy and extremely comical, and in the end we laughed so much that several people stopped to look at us as if they thought we were mad.

When we asked Austin why on earth he was carrying bread in his pockets, he explained gravely that it had been intended for the battalion sow, and that he had had no time to give it to her before catching his train that morning.

In three years of war Austin had been shorn of much of his glory, and was now nothing more romantic than a messing officer in a county regiment engaged on coastal defence. But his enthusiasm for tinned liver, to say nothing of swill, was hardly less than it had originally been for "training". Since the war, possibly for the first time in more than twenty years, he was a happy man, so happy that one forgave him gladly for being rather a bore. The tragedy was that it had taken a world catastrophe to make him into a healthy and reasonably useful member of society, and that in this he was probably by no means unique.

His latest venture was allotments and pig-keeping, and he was nearly as devoted to Biddie the brood sow as he once had been to his pugs. As we fed the ducks he told us all about her and how popular she was and how intelligent. Unofficially, it seemed, she almost ranked as battalion mascot.

One unfortunate incident had occurred however. Shortly after her arrival, she had broken down the gate of her sty and found her way to the cookhouse at an hour when it happened to be empty. By the time the cook discovered her she had eaten the best part of a pound of margarine and a meat loaf intended for tea.

Biddie had a ring through her nose, which was never used because she was so gentle, and the man, losing his temper, seized upon it to haul her out of the hut. Her squeals of agony reached Austin as he was returning to his office from the mess, and he arrived at the cookhouse to find the unfortunate pig being thrust tail first through the doorway, and resisting in a panic of obstinacy. "He twisted that ring so that she bled," Austin told us, his voice shaking with remembered anger. "I . . . I *hit* him . . . twice."

Norrie and I looked at him in amazement, and she asked if he could not be court-martialled for striking a soldier. He smiled slyly. "I thought of that," he said, "before I did it. But there were no witnesses. It would have been his word against mine. Besides I hit him where it wouldn't show." He tossed his last crust to a small black duck. "They all liked old Biddie," he added thoughtfully. "I was quite safe."

Hot heavy raindrops drove us home as darkness fell, Norrie and I to her flat in Knightsbridge, Austin towards his club near Portland Place.

"So like Austin," she remarked as we left him, "that business with the pig, I mean. You think he's an innocent, but he doesn't often do anything without working it out. He told me once when we were children that he never asked father for anything until he had his slippers on, because he used to have corns and sometimes his boots hurt him. I could never have thought up anything like that."

The sirens sounded as we entered the flat. Through the unshaded windows we could see the searchlights pancaked against the low sky, and from the east came the flash and rumble of the guns. Then silence, and the faint droning of engines above the clouds. It was over before we could think of taking cover.

There can only have been one plane, a solitary nuisance raider which managed to dodge the defences. The bombs sounded like four giant footsteps coming nearer and nearer, the last one followed by the sliding crash of masonry. The sky glowed red beyond the roofs of the houses across the street. We heard the fire-engines go past, and then an ambulance. The droning died away. The guns opened up again. Against the distant rumbling the siren on the corner sounded the "All clear."

I was half asleep when the telephone rang in Norrie's bedroom, and I heard her answer. "Yes . . . Yes . . . Oh! Yes . . . where? The Badminton School? Yes. I've got it. Thank you. I'll come at once." I knew what had happened before she came to my door, before I heard her voice, thin and toneless, as she told me the news.

"Come with me, Susan," she said. "He always liked you." In the taxi she held my hand. "I think he's dying," she whispered. I thought so too. We had been enjoying ourselves too much.

"It seems so damned unfair," she said. "He never did any harm to anyone, and he was so pleased at feeling a bit useful." My eyes were pricking with tears, as much for Norrie as for Austin. The dinner we had eaten so happily and the wine we had drunk rose sourly in my throat. "He'll be all right," I said without conviction. "Routine, you know. Informing the next of kin."

"I don't think so," Norrie answered. "They said 'multiple injuries.'"

Austin lay alone in the long school-room at the end of a row of empty beds. The blackout was tight on the windows and the stifling air stank of disinfectants. In the callous light of the one electric bulb the room looked white and grey, bleakly cold for all that it was so hot.

The nurse that brought us to him spoke in a rustling whisper. "Crushed," she said. "Internal hæmorrhage. Too bad to move." I saw Norrie moisten her lips. It seemed so much worse somehow, his being so fat. "A piece of a wall," said the nurse. "The ambulance men said he should have been killed outright."

Austin lay flat in the narrow bed, and the sheets, rumpled in a mound over the dressings on his body, rose and fell with his difficult breathing. His face was grey, sagging, shiny with sweat. It looked queerly featureless, as though it were dissolving into the pillow, fading from the labouring anonymous bulk and the wandering hands.

The nurse wetted his mouth with a swab of cotton. "They're here," she said to him, professionally bright. "You'll feel better now." She whispered to Norrie. "No pain . . . back broken . . . by morning." I saw Norrie wince and moisten her lips again.

Austin opened his eyes. His restless hands groped outwards to find us. "Asthma bad again tonight," he whispered with a smile. We smiled back obediently. Once again he was a hero. For half his life he had fussed over imaginary ills. Now he faced death without fear or complaint.

We sat there watching him, imaginatively stripping the bandages from his body, and feeling on our chests the burden of his breathing. He did not speak; weakness was closing his eyes. But his hands plucked at the coverlet and his head moved restlessly. "Internal bleeding," rustled the nurse. "Always like that." She made us tea, and one at a time we slipped away to drink it.

The night seemed unending. In the sweltering heat I could feel the sweat creep on my skin like tiny insects. At the far end of the room the nurse ate sandwiches and knitted. Every few minutes Norrie bent to sponge Austin's face. I wondered if it made it worse or better for her that she had once been a nurse and knew what wounds and broken bones could look like. A smell was beginning to come from the bed . . . a smell of blood and other things.

"You'd better go out for a while," she said to me. Tears stood in her eyes, though her voice was unconcerned. "He isn't in pain," the nurse whispered, "really he isn't." She offered me a share of her sandwiches, but the idea of food made me feel sick.

I stood on the doorstep and watched while the brooding sky became faintly luminous, and the outlines of the houses shaped themselves darkly against the dawn. A single search-light crossed the sky, waving good-bye to night. It was nearly five o'clock.

Dispassionately I wished poor Austin would hurry up and die, for his own sake and for ours. I wondered what he was thinking of as he lay there. Was he admiring his own courage perhaps? Or did he not know he was dying? Or was he simply too weak to care?

When I went in again Norrie was crying quietly. "He's going soon," she said. Her trained eye could see signs that were invisible to me. He did not seem to be suffering. He lay more like a restless sleeper, moving his head and sighing as he breathed. His eyes opened sometimes, but they seemed not to focus.

Norrie's tears flowed gently, and she made no effort to hold them back. I felt like crying too, not because of Austin, though I had come to like him well enough, but because I was so sorry for her. Her wandering life had left her without close friends. He was probably the only person she really cared for.

He died just before five o'clock, and before he died he spoke. His eyes opened, clear and unclouded. His voice was firm. "I did it with a pillow," he said distinctly. "It was . . . a good idea. Nobody knew . . . not even when I said . . ." His lips curved in the familiar smile, at once childish and sly. His eyes closed again, and the last breath went out of him in a long-drawn sigh.

Norrie stooped and kissed him. "Thank God!" she said.

In the milky light of morning we walked across the park. Norrie had stopped crying and become the practical woman of business. We must wire his unit, she said, and let Mellie know, and see about the undertaker. Yes. She was all right to go to the shop. A bath and a cup of coffee would work wonders. No. No. There was nothing to worry about. Of course not. She sounded almost irritable.

We walked on in silence. Then suddenly, as though the idea had newly struck her, she stopped dead, clutching my arm. "Susan! What did he mean when he talked about a pillow?"

"Oh, nothing." I tried to sound casual while the full meaning of the words prodded my tired brain to wakefulness.

. . . Dodie with the white weals on her black sleek body . . . The girl who had hanged herself in her mother's kitchen . . . Austin, flushed and dishevelled, banging on the dinner table and shouting. . . . Austin's words . . . and Dr Lorton's . . . and all the hundred and one little things I had been told. . . .

"I suppose he was uncomfortable and wanted you to shake it up." My answer sounded silly like the badly told lie it was.

"No," said Norrie. "No. It wasn't that. He said he *did* it with a pillow. And he said . . ."

"He was delirious."

"No. He wasn't. I wonder . . ."

And then she shut her mouth tightly, and when she spoke again she spoke of other things.

THE END

UNTITLED POEM

This is one of Monica Tindall's last poems. Her niece Gillian Tindall arranged to have it read on the BBC ('Poetry Please') in 1994. It was also read aloud at Monica's funeral when she died in spring 1999.

My life is as light as the lightest bird
On the lightest twig at the edge of the world.
Lightly it hangs like a leaf ready to fall
Gently it floats, like paper, shedding its meaning in water.

Strange that my breath still blurs the glass in the window,
And that people can see me coming and hear what I say.
I am no more than a ghost
Hung lightly, lightly
On the hinge of a day.

FURROWED MIDDLEBROW

FM1. *A Footman for the Peacock* (1940) .... RACHEL FERGUSON
FM2. *Evenfield* (1942) .... RACHEL FERGUSON
FM3. *A Harp in Lowndes Square* (1936) .... RACHEL FERGUSON
FM4. *A Chelsea Concerto* (1959) .... FRANCES FAVIELL
FM5. *The Dancing Bear* (1954) .... FRANCES FAVIELL
FM6. *A House on the Rhine* (1955) .... FRANCES FAVIELL
FM7. *Thalia* (1957) .... FRANCES FAVIELL
FM8. *The Fledgeling* (1958) .... FRANCES FAVIELL
FM9. *Bewildering Cares* (1940) .... WINIFRED PECK
FM10. *Tom Tiddler's Ground* (1941) .... URSULA ORANGE
FM11. *Begin Again* (1936) .... URSULA ORANGE
FM12. *Company in the Evening* (1944) .... URSULA ORANGE
FM13. *The Late Mrs. Prioleau* (1946) .... MONICA TINDALL
FM14. *Bramton Wick* (1952) .... ELIZABETH FAIR
FM15. *Landscape in Sunlight* (1953) .... ELIZABETH FAIR
FM16. *The Native Heath* (1954) .... ELIZABETH FAIR
FM17. *Seaview House* (1955) .... ELIZABETH FAIR
FM18. *A Winter Away* (1957) .... ELIZABETH FAIR
FM19. *The Mingham Air* (1960) .... ELIZABETH FAIR
FM20. *The Lark* (1922) .... E. NESBIT

Printed in Great Britain
by Amazon